As Ruth reached the
the green stopped her

'Quick, someone ge

Ruth turned and saw
partners, supporting C....., who siumped heavily against
him. Ruth ran towards them, her heart pounding.

'Is Bill in the clubhouse?' the first man asked Annie.

'No – I'll see if there's anyone else.'

Harris gently lowered Clive to the grass, where he lay
gasping for breath with a deathlike pallor. Ruth knelt
beside him, frantic with fear. 'What happened?' she asked
Harris.

'I don't know. He said he was feeling off. Then he
couldn't get his breath. He just seemed to fold up.'

Jacqueline Osborne

INTIMATE CONTACT

Based on the Central Television series
written by Alma Cullen

SPHERE BOOKS LIMITED

Sphere Books Limited, 27 Wrights Lane, London W8 5TZ

First published in Great Britain by Sphere Books Ltd, 1987

Novelisation copyright © Sphere Books Limited, 1987
based on the television series
INTIMATE CONTACT written by Alma Cullen
Central logo copyright © 1982
Central Independent Television plc.

TRADE
MARK

Set in Sabon

Printed and bound in Great Britain by
Cox & Wyman Ltd, Reading

Chapter 1

On one of the worst days, as Ruth sleepwalked in a valium haze through the nightmare her life had become, she found herself absently dusting the photo and its silver frame. The handsome, successful Gregory family smiled radiantly at the camera, sharing a moment of uncomplicated joy on a momentous occasion. Martin in his cap and gown, beaming with surprised delight that his father had managed to arrive, despite the vicissitudes of weather and flight delays, just in time for the graduation. Clive, exuding vitality, bursting with pride in his firstborn's achievement and pleased with his own logistical genius in co-ordinating company plane and chauffeured limousine with split second timing. Nell, sibling rivalry forgotten for the moment, genuinely happy for her brother and looking so fresh and pretty, so much younger than her eighteen years. And the picture of Ruth herself – could she ever have been that carefree? With excruciating clarity, she recalled the jubilant excitement; the mad dash to meet Clive at the airport; the even wilder dash to the college, she and Nell giggling like schoolgirls while Clive wriggled into fresh clothes in the back seat; the impressive ceremony, the first such she'd attended since Clive's own graduation, that officially confirmed the rite of passage; the garden reception, where graduates and relatives congratulated themselves and each other under a cloudless summer sky. She marvelled at the supreme innocence – or was it simply ignorance? – that had shielded her from intimations of the disaster that was already inexorably under way. They had all been blissfully ignorant, she thought – basking in the bright promise of Martin's political future, Nell's approaching college career, the continuation of the good life, the realisation of their plans and dreams – certainties that had been shattered with such sickening swiftness. Anger rose in her, and tears; expertly, she suppressed both emotions. She replaced the frame on the piano and turned away, but the picture of smiling faces, oblivious to what lay in store, shimmered relentlessly behind her eyes. Maybe one of the children would like to have it, she thought – and went on dusting.

Clive had first misinterpreted, then rationalised and finally dismissed the earliest warning signals. The tiredness was simply, he told himself, a result of over-work. The impotence, unprecedented in his experience, worried him more than he could admit to himself, let alone to Ruth. 'What will you do,' the girl in New York had asked after congratulating him on having the stamina of a young stud, 'when you're too old to get it up any more?'

'Blow my brains out, I suppose.' His laughter had been forced. He was, after all, pushing fifty. A few months later, he wondered whether the girl's remark had been prophetic. The fear was too deep to share even with Bill Stanhope, the new company doctor, who had enquired, off the record, about his health. The Stanhopes were new to the community, but they had joined the golf club almost before they'd unpacked, and Annie Stanhope served with Ruth on the club's women's committee. Martin, always on the lookout for new talent, as he called it, had spotted Sharon Stanhope, their strikingly beautiful daughter, at the club, during his spring break; they'd been an on-and-off item ever since. So there was no reason for Clive to suspect subterfuge when Ruth invited the three

2

Stanhopes around for tea – nor did he suspect anything when Bill took him aside on the pretext of wanting to see his library. The distinguished-looking Stanhope, his grey hair belying his youthful manner, had said casually, 'You mentioned feeling tired.'

'I *am* tired,' Clive replied. 'Wouldn't you be, in the circumstances?'

'So it's no more than ordinary wear and tear?'

'If you can call it ordinary. I've had a hellish two years.'

'I know.'

'Travelling. Setting up the deal. I need a rest.'

'A long rest?'

'No. Couple of weeks in Norfolk for now, as arranged. Usual holidays later.'

'I could get you an extension,' Stanhope offered.

Clive smiled, 'You're a very new company doctor.'

'What does that mean?'

'It means that suggesting an executive take a long rest is the surest way to make him overdo things. How do I look?'

'You look fine to me; the whole board looks like a squash team. Though two of them have had coronaries, I believe. That's what wives worry about.'

'Ah,' said Clive, a light dawning. 'So my wife fixed this?'

'No,' Stanhope lied, embarrassed, 'of course not. But she said that if you mentioned . . .'

Clive nodded. 'I can imagine. A quick word while she showed you the rockery. She fixes most things, Ruth does,' he said admiringly. 'She fixed a company car for Martin's graduation.'

'I heard.'

'Got round the MD.'

'He's been muttering ever since about setting a precedent.'

'Probably thanking God not many kids get Firsts at

Oxford.' He glanced proudly out of the window at Martin, engaged in an uproarious game of croquet with Sharon and Nell at the bottom of the garden.

'I'll take a proper look after your holiday, if you like. Bring your annual check-up forward a bit.'

'You won't need to. Two weeks of fishing in the country and I'll be back on the golf course.'

'Good,' Stanhope said briskly. 'Anything in your notes I should see?'

'No . . . bout of glandular fever in '83.'

'Really? Debilitating, that. Recurs under stress sometimes. It could be our answer.'

'*Her* answer,' said Clive, indicating Ruth, who sat chatting with Annie in the garden.

Ruth saw Clive's gesture and knew instinctively that he was onto her ploy. If it annoyed him, so be it – she'd acted only out of concern for him. If her worries were groundless, so much the better.

Annie Stanhope's voice broke in on Ruth's thoughts. 'We used to drive through this part of town when Bill was a house-surgeon at Bartley General years ago, and I used to say, "One day." He always laughed, of course. Left to himself, he'd've stayed in General Practice all his life. I've had to push.'

Ruth turned her attention to the doctor's wife. The two women were approximately the same age, but the tension in Annie's face and voice made her seem years older. 'We're quite settled in now,' she chatted on, trying too hard. 'Everyone's been marvellous. Between the company and the golf club, we've more invitations than we can cope with. Sharon's never at home, her social life is a real whirl.'

'Moving's such an upheaval,' Ruth said cordially. 'How do you find time for the golf club committee? Not that we're ungrateful, of course – no one wants committee work.'

'Oh, the golf club's a priority,' Annie said earnestly. 'I think you always have to put something in if you want to get something out, don't you?'

'I expect so,' Ruth replied, her mind drifting back towards the men in the library.

'Though I haven't grasped all of the undercurrents yet,' Annie mused.

'Undercurrents?'

'You know — who's stepping out of line, the gossip, that sort of thing. Isn't there a troublemaker somewhere? I thought maybe you'd put me in the picture . . .'

'There isn't even a picture, as far as I know,' Ruth said vaguely. Annie felt the snub, awkwardly cleared her throat and said, 'Well . . . this is all very nice.' No pool, she thought, lowering her estimate of the Gregorys a half-notch. 'We've got drinks with the Fosters after this,' she went on. 'I expect you have, too.'

'No,' said Ruth, 'We haven't, as a matter of fact.'

'Ah,' said Annie, pleased; 'I hope I haven't spoken out of turn.'

'Of course not,' Ruth smiled. 'We just don't see the Fosters.'

'I'm still getting the hang of the social scene,' Annie said ingratiatingly. 'You will "see" us, won't you? I always like to return hospitality. And with Martin and Sharon getting on so well.'

'Yes, of course,' Ruth said warily.

'Although she thought she'd seen the last of him at Easter,' Annie prattled on.

'Really?' What an unpleasant woman, Ruth thought, mentally erasing the Stanhopes from the list on which she'd only just pencilled in their names. 'I can never keep up with the children and their friends.'

'They're more than *friends*, aren't they, those two? Anyway, I hope you'll come and see us sometime. Not that we can aspire to this,' Annie went on, indicating the magnificent, three-storey house and the sumptuous garden. 'You're right out of our league.'

Ruth stood up. 'If you'll excuse me, I'll just get the tea things,' she said coolly, starting towards the house. Annie, now twice snubbed in as many minutes, pointedly remained where she was. Nursing this newest addition to her collection of grievances, she feigned interest in the croquet game at the other end of the garden and strained – in vain – to overhear the children's just-out-of-earshot conversation.

'You're not really going to spend the whole summer electioneering?' Sharon was asking Martin in great dismay. His announcement had been a bombshell and she was trying, not too successfully, to hide her disappointment from him and from his sister, who was indulging her hobby-turned-passion by photographing them from every conceivable angle except standing on her head.

'It won't be the whole summer,' Martin said, his attention on a tricky shot. 'You can help if you like.'

How could he be so casual when he knew how she'd been so looking forward to their planned holiday together? From her very first glimpse of Martin, on the golf course with his father, she'd campaigned single-mindedly for his affection. Tall and well-built, with his mother's colouring – brown hair and eyes, fair complexion – and his father's square jaw and deepset eyes, he was the epitome, she thought, of everything she wanted in a man. Physically, they were wonderfully compatible – they'd established that the very first weekend. With Martin's family background and his success at college, his future glittered auspiciously. Even her mother agreed that he'd be a great catch. 'How can I help you?' she asked dismally. 'It's miles away . . .'

'It's only the next constituency.' He swung his mallet gracefully, gaining another point.

'Maybe she's not a Conservative,' Nell teased.

Sharon addressed Martin, ignoring Nell. 'Mummy's ever

so glad that *you* are. She thinks Oxford and Cambridge make people left-wing.'

'Look,' Martin explained, 'it's a great chance for me, helping Langley.'

'It's not as if he's going to lose, is it?' Sharon argued, knowing it was she who had lost.

'No, but I could work on bumping up his majority.'

'A modest little ambition,' said Nell, her Canon clicking away, 'but what's it got to do with merchant banking?'

'I don't start banking till October,' Martin reminded her. 'Anyway, banking's a stop-gap. I'm a political animal, really.'

'But what about Switzerland?' Sharon asked. She seemed about to cry, but Martin, absorbed in his game, took no notice.

Nell tried to dispel the tension with sarcasm. 'Let him put Britain right first, Sharon . . .'

'You go,' Martin told Sharon, lining up another shot and continuing to ignore her stricken expression. 'There'll be the others—'

'I know, but if you're not there they'll think we—' she couldn't continue. Nell tried again to lighten the mood. 'Why don't you suss out Switzerland for me?' she asked Sharon. 'It's an optional posting if – when – I junk my A-levels. All in French and German. Very wholesome, Switzerland. The discos are like airing cupboards.'

Sharon shot Nell a grateful grin. 'Up to you, Sharon,' said Martin, indicating the croquet ball.

'Did you find the "tea" just a bit strained?' Annie asked her husband as he manoeuvred the car out of the Gregorys' drive.

'Is that a pun?'

'Don't be clever. "Tea" mind you – not lunch. Not dinner. No other guests – I think we've been placed.'

'Is that how it works?'

'You know that's how it works. It was a duty invitation to a company employee on the next rung down. I'd rather she hadn't bothered.'

'She probably wouldn't have bothered if she hadn't been worried. No board member has a duty to the company doctor.'

'Although . . . we *are* new neighbours . . .'

'Not close enough, however.'

'And there's Sharon . . .'

'I'm not entirely happy about that. He uses her, that boy. And I didn't like the way she said she'd stay overnight. Pointed. She should've left with us.'

'By the look of things, we've all been used,' Annie said, resentfully. 'Still, at least you told Ruth what she wanted to hear.'

'Convincing, was I?'

Annie gave him a sharp glance. 'Is there something wrong?'

Bill shrugged. 'Wives have a way of being the first to know.'

'She'd cope if she had to,' Annie reflected. 'Coping's her style. "Are there any leagues?" "There isn't even a picture".'

Years of practice had made Stanhope an expert at tuning his wife out. Alone in his thoughts, he drove on.

Although Ruth enjoyed the intimacy of sex with her husband, she had never considered the act essential. Clive's impotence would have been irrelevant, perhaps even a relief to her, had it not been so obviously distressing to him. Lying in bed beside him after still another false start, she said, 'Did you tell Bill Stanhope about this?'

Clive hesitated. 'Not specifically. Why should I?'

'You said you talked . . .'

'We did, in general terms. I wasn't going to *tell* him . . . It's only an effect of the whole thing, Ruth. It'll go.'

'I wish,' she said impulsively, 'you'd have an examination.'

He shifted his position, moving slightly away from her. 'Oh, come on, Ruth – since when has this been such a big deal for you, anyway?'

'What?' she asked, defensive.

'This. Bed. Sex.'

He was probing at a nerve now. 'What do you mean?' she asked anxiously. 'I've always welcomed you . . .'

'I can't imagine you're feeling unbearably frustrated.'

His sarcasm stung, and put an edge on her response: 'Are *you*?'

'Look,' he said evading the question 'The heat's off now. The New York deal's tied up. I'll get some proper rest in Norfolk . . .'

'There's still the demonstration,' she reminded him.

'No problem. It'll go like clockwork.'

Hesitantly, Ruth voiced her secret fear. 'It isn't – it isn't me, is it?'

Clive felt a twinge of remorse; whatever was wrong, it wasn't fair to take it out on Ruth, who was as conscientious about sex as she was about running the house. 'Listen,' he said placatingly, 'when's this silver wedding coming off? Six, seven weeks?'

She smiled 'You know perfectly well . . .'

'It'll be terrific by then,' he promised. 'Like a ram. You'll wish you'd never said a word. It'll be better than our honeymoon. Though, as I remember, anything'd be better than that!'

She squirmed inwardly at the memory. 'Well, if you would have a twenty-year-old virgin . . .'

'There was nothing else then, was there?' Was it his imagination, or could he actually hear Martin going at it with Sharon upstairs, just over his head? He glanced at

Ruth, who gave no sign. 'Doesn't it give you a pang,' he asked. 'seeing how the young manage it today? Martin strolling upstairs with his girl . . .'

'It doesn't give *me* a pang.'

'No?'

'No.' She turned and kissed him affectionately. 'I got exactly what I wanted.'

Wearily, Clive shut his eyes and tried to think about what was most certainly going on in Martin's bedroom.

Chapter 2

Naked, Clive Gregory regarded his image in the bedroom mirror with satisfaction. He was a large well-built man, just over six feet, with the broad shoulders of the oarsman he'd been in his youth and the rock-hard belly of the squash player he was today. Only the slightly receding hairline and few grey hairs – imperceptible, he assured himself – betrayed the fact that in two years he'd be fifty. Pulling on jeans and a sweatshirt for the drive to Norfolk, he repeated to himself what he'd said to Ruth: two weeks in the country and he'd be good as new.

Clive ordinarily dreaded holidays; he much preferred to work. He loved his job – loved the challenge of it, thrived on the stress and the power games. He considered himself living proof that a shopkeeper's son could rise to the rarefied echelons of top management if he was intelligent, personable, and willing to work as hard as the job demanded. He acknowledged that luck was a small but significant factor. It was luck that he'd chosen electronics as his field at precisely the right time, when the industry was in its infancy and opportunities wide open. His aptitude had been evident from the start; in each of the four companies he'd worked for during his business career, he had ascended the corporate ladder without a miss-step, acquiring the accoutrements of status and success along the way. His present job, in which he and his team had developed a multi-million-pound state-of-the-art system, suited him perfectly. He believed that every problem had a solution. He believed in cause and effect.

11

He believed in order. Science was orderly. His life was orderly. Messiness, if not quite a sin, was inexcusable.

Finding a wife like Ruth had perhaps been his greatest luck. She was a superb administrator; she understood the importance of order and planning. He gave her full marks for running the house as efficiently as he ran his management team. She never complained about the frequent absences his job entailed; returning from a business trip, he could always count on finding the house immaculate, the children healthy and well-behaved, expenditures well within the limits he set. She tended their image in the community as carefully as she tended the flower beds; she was a stalwart member of the golf club women's committee, a tireless volunteer at the local Oxfam shop, and never refused a request to help out with a charity event. He took particular pride in her appearance; she had managed to keep her face, with its delicate features, and her figure looking far younger than her forty-six years. She entertained his clients with unfailing *savoir faire*, always wearing and saying exactly the right thing. She had never bothered him with the hiccups of running the household, even though he knew things couldn't always have ticked along as smoothly as she made them appear. And if she'd never been particularly enthusiastic about sex – well, she wasn't that kind of woman, was she? If she were, he couldn't respect her the way he did. She was a kind, gentle woman – a good wife, as he was a good husband – good provider, generous, fair, and reasonably faithful. He couldn't help it if women found him attractive. He'd never claimed to be a saint.

The day after the Gregorys returned from Norfolk – two days before Clive's scheduled return to work – Clive and Ruth arrived at the golf course together. He had arranged a game with two company colleagues; she was expected at a meeting of the women's committee. Watching her husband as he walked towards the green, Ruth's concern showed on her face. Norfolk had not lived up to expectation. Clive had gone fishing every day, but it was obvious to her that he'd have preferred to stay in bed. She bought vitamin supplements, which, to her surprise, he swallowed without argument. At the end of the fortnight, he'd agreed to have an examination as soon as he got back to work.

As Ruth turned towards the club house, a figure emerged and ran towards her – the last person she wanted to see.

'Thank God you've arrived, Ruth,' said an agitated Annie Stanhope. 'How was Norfolk?'

'Fine,' said Ruth, noncommittal.

'And Clive?'

'All right. Still tired.' She moved towards the clubhouse. 'Is anything wrong?'

'Yes, as a matter of fact. There's been a bit of an incident. I don't think I need to say who . . .'

Ruth was in no mood for games: 'I think you do.'

'I think I've been here long enough to know there's only one troublemaker in this place,' Annie said spitefully. 'Anyhow, we were just arranging the committee room when the bar steward came in and said he absolutely refused to serve—'

'Don't you dare!' a husky female voice called out from the clubhouse. Ruth turned to see a dishevelled redhead swaying drunkenly down the clubhouse steps, clinging to a hapless man at least twenty years her senior. Ruth knew Becca Crichton from the women's committee, but only casually. 'Don't you dare tell on me,' Becca shouted at Annie. 'I'll do my own talking!'

'Someone's sent for a taxi,' Annie whispered to Ruth as Becca approached.

'Foiled!' Becca announced to whomever might be within earshot. 'Foiled!' To Annie she said, 'Lost your nerve did you? Ran for the sheriff?'

'Are you leaving, Becca?' Ruth asked calmly.

Becca grinned tipsily at her escort, who smiled weakly back. 'You bet. I'm leaving with him. He of the silver-buttoned blazer. Mistake on a man of his age, really. Still, he tottered across a crowded room and whispered, "Can I drop you somewhere?" So how could I resist? Although "drop" isn't the happiest choice of words, seeing as how I can't get much lower than this.'

'I'll cancel the taxi, then . . .' Annie moved towards the clubhouse, but Becca blocked her way.

'Who asked for a taxi, anyway?' She stared searchingly at Annie. 'Tell Ruth what you said, in a loud voice, when I came in. About a certain member and his wife.'

'I simply asked,' Annie said righteously, 'why we never see Eddie Doran's wife at the club. She's on the list. And . . .' She lowered her eyes, embarrassed.

'. . . and was it really because she lost her husband to another member?'

Ruth decided that the situation had deteriorated quite far enough. 'Go home, Becca,' she said, firm but not unfriendly.

'Sorry,' Annie murmured. 'I put my foot in it. I'm new here.'

'Eddie Doran was not *lost* by his wife,' Becca said belligerently. 'He was mis*laid*. Whereas *I* laid him good and proper! While it lasted.'

'Come on,' said her now miserable escort, pushing her in the direction of his car.

'That's what I like about him,' Becca called back. 'His impatience.' As he virtually shoved her into the car, they heard her ask, 'What's your name?'

Ruth turned to Annie, feeling obliged to defend Becca. 'She lost custody of her children after the divorce. After that she seemed to stop caring about . . . everything.'

'I think she should go on this afternoon's agenda,' said Annie, righteousness regained.

'The agenda's been decided.'

Annie was adamant: 'I know I'd have support.'

'This is an irregular conversation,' Ruth shot back. 'I believe the meeting may have started already.' She walked purposefully towards the clubhouse. As he reached the steps, a shout from the direction of the green stopped her in her tracks.

'Quick, someone get a doctor!' a man yelled.

Ruth turned and saw Geoff Harris, one of Clive's golf partners, supporting Clive, who slumped heavily against him. Ruth ran towards them, her heart pounding.

'Is Bill in the clubhouse?' the first man asked Annie.

'No – I'll see if there's anyone else.'

Harris gently lowered Clive to the grass, where he lay gasping for breath with a deathlike pallor. Ruth knelt beside him, frantic with fear. 'What happened?' she asked Harris.

'I don't know. He said he was feeling off. Then he couldn't get his breath. He just seemed to fold up.'

Ruth took Clive's hand and helplessly patted it, heedless of the crowd that was gathering around them. 'It's all right, darling,' she lied, terrified that every breath could be Clive's last. Someone said 'Look's like a hospital job'; someone else backed a car up onto the grass and two men helped Clive into the back seat, where he lay heavily against Ruth. Minutes later, Clive was being carried into a private clinic on a stretcher.

Ruth waited in a corridor, wondering whether her husband was dead or alive – and afraid to ask.

Three days later, Ruth knew little more than that Clive *was* alive, and that some of the most obvious possible diagnoses had been ruled out. He'd been moved to the nearest provincial NHS hospital, about fifteen miles away, because, Bill Stanhope explained, they could do more tests there. He suspected viral pneumonia. 'Don't worry,' he'd told her. *Don't worry?* Clive was the centre of her life – even more so than the children. *Don't worry?* She tried, nonetheless, to carry on as normal, to concentrate on domestic minutiae. For three days she cleaned, cooked, shopped and weeded the garden as though her life depended on it; if she could keep that part of her life normal, perhaps the rest would remain normal as well. She concealed the extent of her concern from the children so expertly that Nell seemed more worried about her A-level results than about her father. 'If the results from Dad's tests are okay,' she remarked hopefully, 'he ought to be merciful if mine aren't all that he'd hoped, don't you think? I mean, he can't have everything.'

On the third afternoon, while Ruth polished her already sparkling silver with the grudging help of her daily, Mrs Gordon, the phone call she'd awaited with impatient dread finally came. An hour later she was in the foyer of the huge NHS hospital, trying to remember the directions to Clive's room, when she heard Bill Stanhope call her name. 'I'm a bit lost in this place,' she said, grateful to see him. 'How is he?'

'Let's go straight up, shall we,' said Bill, his face drawn with concern. 'The bloody lift's just gone; shall we walk up?'

'Have you seen him?' Ruth asked, alarmed by his gravity.

'They wouldn't let me. The specialist was with him.' He climbed the stairs ahead of Ruth, his face averted.

'Isn't that routine?'

'I don't know. I don't know what the bloody routine is in these places. It's all bloody National Health bureaucracy.'

'But Clive's all right?'

'They're not saying.'

'He seemed all right when I talked to him last night,' Ruth said, telling herself what she needed to hear.

'Was he?'

'Well, he was . . . just the same.'

'Whatever that means,' Stanhope muttered.

They'd reached the top of the stairs; Ruth grabbed his arm and asked fearfully, 'What's going on, Bill?'

'Ask *them* what's going on,' he said, starting down the corridor, still avoiding her eyes. 'Ask Clive.'

She strained to keep up. 'Clive?'

'You'll be told,' Bill said resentfully. 'I won't.

'Surely the consultant will tell you,' Ruth said, bewildered. 'Won't he? Do you know him?'

At the end of the corridor, Bill turned to face her at last. The mixture of horror and fear on his face made her gasp. 'Not personally,' he said ominously, 'but I know what he specialises in.'

He opened a door, through which Ruth saw a youngish doctor, owlish in hornrim spectacles, who walked towards her. 'Mrs Gregory?' he said, extending his hand. 'I'm Trevor Singleton, consultant in charge of this unit. Please come in. Dr Stanhope can wait for you outside.'

Behind Singleton, huddled in a chair in dressing gown and pyjamas, was a Clive Ruth scarcely recognised. He looked shrunken, desperately ill, with an expression of pure anguish on his face. Dreading something she couldn't have named, Ruth stepped hesitantly into the room.

Chapter 3

'This is what I'm going to do, Mrs Gregory,' Singleton said as he shut the door. She was shaking. 'Mrs Gregory?'

Pull yourself together, she admonished herself, and found her voice. 'Yes?'

'I'm going to leave you to talk to your husband for a few minutes, and then I'm going to come back and speak to both of you. I'll be in the next room, if you need me.' He opened the door to the adjoining room.

Clive spoke pleadingly to Singleton: 'I don't think I can do this.'

'We agreed it was the best way,' said the consultant. Clive nodded assent.

Singleton stepped through the doorway; the door closed behind him.

Ruth stood frozen, wanting to cross the room and comfort her husband but unable to move. 'What is it?' she asked. 'What have they found? It's bad, isn't it?'

Clive looked at the floor; his voice, when he finally spoke, was a muffled croak. 'Listen, Ruth,' he began, but couldn't continue. He looked close to tears.

'Whatever it is, we'll face it,' she said. 'We'll face it together. Now tell me—'

'I have to tell you some other things first,' Clive said in the same strange, unfamiliar voice. 'I'm going to hurt you . . . and disgust you . . .'

Her face went blank with incomprehension. Haltingly, Clive continued. 'Remember, eighteen months ago, one

18

of the first trips to New York on this deal? And how we weren't hopeful, didn't think we could bring it off?'

'Yes,' Ruth said, nodding encouragement.

'But we did bring it off, me and the team, against all the odds. We brought it off. We celebrated – I told you. There was a party. We joined up with another group at the hotel, went to somebody's room. Somebody had the idea of bringing in a floor show – just a few rough-looking girls, really, who did a bit of pathetic dancing and stripping. We were drunk, stupid. There was a bit of horseplay. The girls were tarts, really, of course – practised. In the end, we all joined in . . . and ended up in bed, got taken for a ride. Seems it's the usual sort of thing.' He paused, searching for words. Ruth waited, trembling. 'She gave me something, that girl . . .'

'Gave you something?'

'Yes. Left me with something. She must've been filthy, rotten, diseased . . .'

'Do you mean . . .' Ruth began, comprehension dawning, 'it's some kind of . . .'

'Listen,' Clive said, forcing the words out, still unable to look at her. 'I'm going to say it once and then I'll never say it again. It's AIDS. That's what I've got. Do you know what it is?'

Ruth backed against a table for support. 'What?' she asked, trying to take in the inconceivable.

'You heard me! You heard me! I won't say it again! I'll never say it again.'

Ruth took a step backward, away from Clive. 'It . . . it can't be! It can't! I've read about it. It's only—'

'It isn't,' Clive broke in, weeping. 'It isn't only queers who get it. *I've* got it! Me! They've done the tests. And . . . it's active.'

'Active?'

'I've got six months.' Exhausted, sobbing, he sank back into his chair.

19

Ruth held out her arms, wanting to go to him, but her feet wouldn't move. 'Clive darling – we've got to think – there's a way of dealing with—' was all she could manage before a spasm of deep-seated revulsion that outweighed her sympathy caught at her throat and made her retch.

Calmer but still distraught after the attack of nausea subsided, Ruth sat in a chair next to Clive's, trying to take in Dr Singleton's words. 'It's my experience that you'll have nothing worse to face than this, if that helps. Now, at this point I'm simply going to talk. Interrupt if you like. Ask questions, or just listen.' Clive reached for Ruth's hand; she moved it away. Singleton watched them both carefully. 'For the moment,' he went on, 'let's knock out blame, shall we? Let's say that the problem exists, now, and consider what we're going to do about it. Okay?'

'Okay,' Clive murmured. Ruth nodded.

'Fine. In the short term, I'd expect Clive to become rather more acutely ill than he is right now. He's been incubating the virus for about a year and a half, and he's entering the first stages of a pneumonia that's going to pull him down a bit over the next week or two. But we can get him better from that and send him home. A short convalescence and then he can go back to work, providing it's not too taxing—'

'Jesus,' Clive broke in, 'I'll *give* it to people!'

'You won't. Believe me. Think: if it could be caught that easily, I'd be dead.' He paused, letting the information sink in. 'It's spread only through contact of the most intimate sort. Homosexuals are most at risk, as you probably know, and your prostitute carrier had almost certainly got it from a bisexual subject; or she may have been a high-risk heroin addict. Drug addicts can get it from sharing a needle with a carrier. Or perhaps she had contaminated sperm from someone else in her body when—'

Ruth gasped, seemed about to retch again, but re-covered.

'Sorry,' Singleton apologised. 'I'm just airing the pos-sibilities. Cases of female to male infection are extremely rare, as far as we know. We're still learning; the picture changes practically every day. All we know for certain is that it's on the rampage.'

'You mean I was unlucky,' Clive said bitterly.

'Everyone who gets AIDS is unlucky – like everyone who gets hepatitis, or tuberculosis. I have to ask this,' Singleton said, clinical but not cold: 'What form of birth control have you used?'

'I gave up the pill three years ago,' Ruth said, 'after the scare. Since then . . .'

'I've taken care of it,' Clive said.

'You mean sheaths?'

'Yes.'

'Good; then the risk to your wife is negligible. We'll do a test as a precaution.'

'The children?' Clive asked.

'No risk at all.'

Ruth spoke in a harsh, angry, hopeless voice that she'd never used before. 'That's what they'll think you are. They'll say you're really a queer.'

Clive looked at her blankly, drained of emotion.

'Who are "they", Mrs Gregory?' Singleton asked, making no effort to hide his distaste. 'And why should they be told?'

Bill Stanhope was pacing the corridor, impatient and anxious, when Singleton finally emerged from Clive's room. 'When am I going to be let in on this?' the com-pany doctor asked.

Singleton started down the corridor towards his office, Stanhope right behind him. 'Let in?' the consultant re-peated.

'You have my patient in there!'

Singleton observed him coolly. 'In what sense is he your patient?'

'What?' asked Stanhope, thrown by the unexpected challenge.

'I'm under no obligation to inform a company doctor about his condition,' Singleton said matter-of-factly. 'All the relevant notes will go to his GP.'

'He never sees his GP,' Stanhope protested. 'I doubt if he'd know him! He travels a great deal – men like him can't go through the appointments system, they've no time. That's why the company employs me.'

'I daresay. Nonetheless, that's the position.'

Increasingly agitated, Stanhope followed the consultant into his office. 'You can't do this!' he said indignantly. 'There may be other people involved!'

'I doubt it.'

'I know you're a venereologist,' Stanhope said contentiously. 'I've seen your stuff in the journals.'

'If you've read it, as opposed to just having "seen" it, you'll know there's no cause for panic.'

'What is it?' Stanhope whispered conspiratorially, one member of the medical club to another. 'Syphillis? That's what I thought it was.' Singleton's expression betrayed nothing. 'Is it . . . AIDS?' Stanhope asked, uttering the unthinkable. 'It's AIDS, isn't it – or you wouldn't have been brought in so quickly.'

'I've said no discussion,' Singleton stonewalled.

'The other men,' Stanhope spluttered, his panic rising. 'The management team – they'll have to be checked! Right away! Blood tests! Christ, some of them are on holiday, like Clive! Get them traced – I have to make a phone call . . .' He reached for the telephone on the desk.

'No, you don't.' Singleton slammed his hand down on the receiver. 'If it's what you think it is, you'll do no good. The chances of anyone else being infected are minute. It's *extremely* difficult to catch,' he said emphatically. 'All you'll do is spread panic and get your patient ostracised.'

'It's more than my job's worth,' Stanhope muttered.

Singleton was unimpressed. 'Cushy number, that. Company doctor.'

'Listen,' Stanhope remonstrated, 'I've got to live in the real world.'

'Where do you think *I* live?' the consultant asked. 'You should take a ward with me some time.' He spoke earnestly, without rancour. 'Do nothing. Say nothing.'

'The medical certificate?'

'Leave that to me. Now, I've taken the liberty of telling Mrs Gregory that you'll drive her home. She'll be waiting downstairs.'

Shaken and dazed, Ruth waited for Stanhope in the hospital foyer. In the car, he groped vainly for words; the silence tightened until, nearly at their destination, Stanhope felt he had to break it. 'Perhaps you'd be more comfortable staying at a friend's house tonight,' he suggested.

She answered vaguely, sounding dazed. 'No. Thanks, Bill. I must go home. Martin said he'd ring.'

'Electioneering, is he?' Stanhope grasped at the conversational straw. 'Sharon cried off today when she saw the rain. Her hair. I pulled her leg, said her political commitment was a bit weak. Oh, God,' he burst out, the pretence of normality breaking down, 'this is terrible, isn't it? Horrendous!'

She glanced over at him, but said nothing until he had turned the car into the drive and brought it to a stop at her front door. When she did speak, her words were almost dreamy. 'I was thinking this morning how lovely the house looks. How glad I was I'd got it painted before the party.'

Stanhope was nonplussed. 'Party?'

'We'll have been married twenty-five years in September. We'll go ahead with the party, of course.' Stanhope gaped, speechless. 'He'll be home by then. The consultant said he'd be home in three weeks. I don't want Clive to miss anything, any fun. I want him to enjoy everything, to the very last possible minute.'

Stanhope was incredulous. 'Have you thought what you're going to tell people—' he caught himself – 'I mean, the children? About Clive?'

She looked directly at him for the first time. 'I'll tell them the truth, of course.'

'The *truth*?'

'Yes,' she said, as though merely stating the obvious. 'That's he's got cancer.'

'Cancer?' It was a challenge to which Stanhope couldn't respond.

'Yes,' Ruth said firmly. 'That's what it is. I thought you realised.'

As she opened the car door, Nell emerged from the house. *She looks so normal*, Ruth thought. *Everything looks so normal*. With a great effort of will, she got out of the car. Nell greeted her with an apprehensive smile. 'If there's any justice in the world,' she said, 'Dad should've got off lightly. Because I didn't. Disaster.' She handed Ruth a piece of paper.

'What is it?' Ruth asked, fighting for control.

'Failed my A-levels,' Nell said lightly. 'Told you.'

Ruth put an arm around her daughter's shoulders. 'We have to get the spare room ready for Daddy,' she said, and gently led her indoors.

Breathing with difficulty, Clive had watched from the hospital window as Stanhope helped Ruth into the car, got behind the wheel and drove out of the car park. Ruth had looked up in his direction, her expression blurred by the falling rain. If she'd seen him, she'd given no indication. Behind him, a nurse said, 'Back into bed now, Mr Gregory.'

He climbed into the bed, using his last ounce of energy, and lay motionless, eyes closed, while the nurse arranged the bedcovers over him. He heard Singleton's voice: 'You'll be wanting to stay there for a while. That's the usual pattern.'

Clive lifted his eyelids; they felt like lead. 'I don't want to know the usual pattern,' he said contemptuously.

'We run a counselling service here . . .' Singleton began, sensing potential trouble.

'Counselling's for people who can't take responsibility for themselves. That's never been my problem.'

'Your wife, perhaps, under the strain . . .'

'She feels the same.'

'If you change your mind . . .'

'I'd like to be alone if you don't mind,' Clive said. He shut his eyes again. In a moment, he heard the door close quietly.

Ruth's reaction had been made no less painful by its predictability; if there was such a thing as Divine Retribution, watching the loving concern in her eyes change to revulsion and horror had surely been more punishment than anyone could deserve.

His body was weak, but his mind was racing. For the hundredth time since he'd been given the diagnosis, he tried to remember the details of that night in the New York hotel room. There'd been nothing particularly memorable about it, except that the victory they were celebrating had been, ironically, the most resounding of his career. If the deal had fallen through, they'd probably have had the same party, but to console, rather than congratulate, one another. After two years of concentrated effort, wasn't a man entitled to break loose?

His girl had been unusually young, probably no older than Nell, he'd thought at the time – not that a whore like that could have anything in common with his daughter *except* her age. He couldn't even remember her name. She'd been a hot little redhead – hot enough that in spite of all the gin inside him, he'd managed it twice, with Geoff, Paddy and the others cheering him on after *their* girls had left them begging for mercy. It had been a *party*, for Christ's sake – nothing more or less. Just another run-of-the-mill party – or so it had seemed at the time. A bit of well-deserved fun after the long, gruelling push. In the light of the consequences, he could imagine nothing more squalid. Wracked with rage, shame and self-loathing, he turned his face to the wall.

Other people's bad news always gave Annie Stanhope a little lift, and she was feeling one now. Not that she would have *wished* the tragedy of cancer on the Gregorys, of course. As she told Bill while she cleared away the supper dishes, 'I don't want to warm to Ruth, but I do admire her, in a way. If I were in her position, I'd go to pieces. But Ruth – you've got to hand it to her. She'll cope. She'll be wonderful. The way she copes on the committee, and in the Oxfam shop. If anyone can save Clive, she will. I'll write her a little note.'

'She can't save him,' Bill said, pouring himself another large whisky. He'd stopped at the pub on the way home, and had been drinking seriously ever since.

'You've had cancer patients with that prognosis before,' Annie reminded him. He shook his head. 'Yes you have! Given six months and lived five years. Longer, some of them.'

Bill sighed. 'Not this time.'

'Why not?'

'He's dead, Annie. As good as.'

The last dishes cleared away, Annie sat down opposite her husband. 'Well,' she said philosophically, 'that puts it all in perspective, doesn't it? All their success.'

'Yes,' he said, his voice thick with drink and irony, 'what's success, after all? What's it brought *us*, for instance? Only a big house in a nice neighbourhood, and three cars, and a swimming pool. And a lot of hairdressing, and drink, and travel. You wouldn't want to lose any of that, though, would you?'

She frowned, taken aback by his tone. 'I meant, compared with good health—'

'Even bad health's easier if you're not short of a few bob, isn't it?'

'Then they'll be all right from that point of view, won't they? What's the matter?' she asked, puzzled. 'Why *should* we lose it?'

'If there's any trouble over this . . .' Bill began, saying more than he intended and slightly slurring his words, ' . . . It's a powerful company. A lot of influence. If I don't handle it properly . . .'

'Handle *what*?'

' . . . I could be back in general practice – if they'd have me, at my age. Or locum work again: stinking houses, stinking people. . . . And he wasn't completely straight with me, he couldn't have been . . . *nor* that so-called expert . . .'

Annie gave her husband a searching look. 'Have you told me everything?'

Instead of replying, he poured himself another drink. Annie, who knew how to get information out of her husband, was poised to attack when their daughter appeared in the doorway, saying, 'I've just spoken to Martin on the phone.'

'How is he?' her mother asked.

'The hospital said no visitors apart from Ruth. The treatment's pretty gruesome, apparently. Poor old Mart. He's wiped out. Ruth wants him to be normal, go back on the campaign. I said I'll stick it out with him.'

'You'll be in Switzerland,' Bill said emphatically.

She shook her head. 'I'm going to cancel.'

'Oh no, you're not.'

'Why not?' Sharon and Annie asked in unison.

'Because it'll get morbid and unhealthy, all that. I *know*. Stay out of it.

'I can't stay away from *Martin*,' Sharon protested.

'Yes, you can,' her father said, pounding the table. 'You *should*, anyway.'

'Stop it, Bill,' Annie said alarmed.

'Christ,' Bill growled angrily, 'you weren't hoping for a wedding, were you?' His daughter was white with dismay. 'You've slept with him, haven't you? Had sex?'

'I don't want to talk about it,' Sharon gasped, on the verge of tears. 'You've no right – you've no right!'

'Go to bed, Sharon,' Annie told her. Weeping, the girl ran out of the room.

Stanhope drained his glass, then buried his head in his hands. 'All right, Bill,' his wife said quietly. 'Let's have it.' He raised his head to meet her penetrating stare.

Chapter 4

Annie had assessed Ruth correctly; she did cope, but at a cost Annie would never imagine. She had always disapproved of tranquillisers; now she depended on Valium for sleep and for sanity, although not even the medication could dissolve the knot in her stomach, or dispel the feeling of dread with which she awoke each morning before dawn. Sometimes she managed to get through the motions of her normal routine by pretending Clive was just away on a business trip. Sometimes she simply sat staring at space, trying to absorb the aftershocks. She had no confidante; she'd never needed one. Instead of friends, she had social acquaintances. Her family had never been close, geographically or emotionally. She and her brother, who now lived in New Zealand, had attended boarding schools while their mother accompanied their father, a career Army officer, on his various postings.

Clive's assessment of her was also correct: like him, she believed that people were responsible for the consequences of their actions. But surely she'd done nothing to deserve this! It was Clive's actions who had wrecked her life, along with his own – not to mention the children's. He had betrayed them, betrayed her, and everything she valued. Viewed in hindsight, the extent of her naivety made her cringe. The pain of his deception was compounded by her realisation of her own self-deception.

Sex had always been on the periphery of her world. Now it was at the centre, tearing it apart. A product of

29

her class and time, she had clamped a lid on her sexuality long before she'd met Clive. She had never heard her mother utter the word 'sex', but the subliminal message had been unmistakable: sex was dirty. Even nice people had to do it sometimes, but they never talked about it. Married love was spiritual; the physical side was a necessary evil.

At boarding school she'd acquired a considerable amount of sex education, almost all of it inaccurate. She had never questioned the double standard of the day, accepting that virginity was not only necessary but desirable for her until marriage – but not for Clive, who she knew had had what she'd dimly thought of as 'experience' before their chaste courtship. Men were like that, her mother had said; they had 'drives' and 'needs' that women couldn't understand. They were all after the same thing, but if you didn't get them to marry you first, they wouldn't marry you afterwards. Her mother had stopped short of telling her to close her eyes and think of England, but that was the implication.

She had never doubted Clive's faithfulness, not for one moment. Even when friends' husbands had strayed – one of the euphemisms with which they masked their squeamishness – she'd always felt, if not smugly superior, grateful for the solidity of her own marriage, based on unshakeable trust and honesty. Had Clive been laughing at her all that time? She tried to think of little signals she might have missed: unexplained phone calls, lipstick on his collar, the clues of which second-rate melodramas are made. The dying man in the hospital room was a stranger. The Clive she'd known, or thought she'd known – the Clive with whom she'd shared more than half her life – was already dead.

And yet . . . in the depth of her anger and despair, she coped. She told the children the cancer story, hating Clive for putting her in the position of having to hurt them as she'd been hurt. They took it as well as could be expected, asking surprisingly few questions and expressing a degree of concern for her that moved her to tears. Her emotions had never been so close to the surface; resolutely, she pushed them down. *No more tears*, she told herself; they did no one any good.

They all coped, in their respective fashions. Martin immersed himself in the election campaign, keeping himself too busy to think. Nell spent her days shooting photographs, evenings working in her improvised dark-room. Mercifully numbed by the Valium, Ruth settled into a routine that was a parody of normalcy – keeping the house going, thanking callers for their flowers and sympathy, driving to and from the hospital every day on automatic pilot, in a dangerous daze. By tacit agreement, she and Clive behaved as though the viral pneumonia was their only problem; their conversations were superficial and stilted. The consultant assured them that thanks to Clive's general fitness before the illness struck, he was more than holding his own.

At the end of the second week, Ruth was following the now-familiar path through the hospital grounds when she noticed unusual activities under way: colourful stalls being set up, balloons and banners flying, a majorette troupe rehearsing and a brass band tuning up. Making her way through the crowd of people bustling to and fro, she heard a husky voice call her name. She turned to see a woman she couldn't immediately identify.

'It's Becca,' the woman prompted, laughing. 'Hello, Ruth. I'm getting to be unrecognisable when I'm sober. How're things?'

Becca had a penchant for colourful clothes; today, her rainbow-hued print dress suited the occasion. 'Not so good,' Ruth replied.

'Ah, I'm sorry.'

'Life goes on,' Ruth said.

'Yes. That's the shittiest thing about life, isn't it?'

Taken aback, Ruth changed the subject. 'What's happening here?'

'It's the hospital carnival, God help us . . .'

Of course, Ruth thought – she'd often helped out at similar affairs herself. 'Are you involved?'

'Marginally. I'm with that lot.' Becca nodded in the direction of two nurses who were supervising a group of children, most of them in wheelchairs. 'We've come to see the horses.'

'I didn't think you helped out here,' Ruth said, surprised.

'Other way round. They help *me* out. That's the idea. It's called emotional transfer, I believe, in alcoholic circles.'

'Is that official?' Ruth asked, uncertain quite how to respond.

'What, me as an alcoholic? Well, I'm still reading the handbooks to see if I qualify. The lawyers say that unless I acknowledge the problem and take steps to deal with it, I can forget reapplying for custody. So here I am, dealing with it.' A small boy who had detached himself from the group pulled at Becca's skirt, demanding to be picked up. 'Mind you, it can feel like penance.' She patted the child's head affectionately. 'This one's just bitten a majorette on the thigh. Do you think that's sex or hunger?'

Ruth smiled. 'I must go.'

'Give Clive my best.' Ruth nodded and turned away. 'I don't suppose I'll see you at the trial?' Becca called after her.

Ruth turned back. 'Trial?'

'I'm up before the golf club committee next Thursday. To give an account of myself.'

'I didn't know,' Ruth said. 'I've . . . been away.'

'The letter says things like "We're not unaware of mitigating circumstances". I think I'll plead guilty and bow out.'

Ruth recognised the bravado, and sympathised. 'Don't do that,' she said. 'I'll try and be there.'

'Okay,' Becca said gratefully. They exchanged rueful smiles, and Ruth turned once again toward G block in the huge hospital complex.

Singleton stood at the end of Clive's bed, looking down at his patient. Clive lay on his back – listless, pale, depressed. The consultant was feeling pretty depressed himself these days; he was long overdue for a holiday, but the work load kept increasing and there simply weren't enough staff to keep up. He was bone-tired – not only from the long hours, but from helplessly witnessing the inevitable decline and death of his patients, many of them younger than himself. This hellish virus – the very word came, appropriately, from the Latin meaning slimy liquid, poison, stench. The only relief from the grim picture was the courage of some of his patients. Their reactions to the diagnosis ran the gamut, from suicidal rage to philosophical acceptance. Singleton tried never to judge his patients – he was, God knows, unequivocally their ally – but he couldn't help wondering sometimes why it was that those most in need of counselling tended to be the ones who most adamantly refused it. Gregory was taking it worse than most, stolidly suppressing his anger and frustration, wallowing in guilt and self-pity. Perhaps he'd had more to lose – although, in actual fact, all of them lost everything in the end. Gregory seemed ready to give up – while his wife, whose relentlessly cheerful manner Singleton found more irritating each time he saw her, seemed to fear the *embarrassment* of her husband's condition even more than his impending death.

But when Ruth entered the room and Singleton saw again how the strain of the past week had ravaged her face – the tension in her jaw, the terror in her eyes – he chided himself for his lack of compassion. 'Hello,' she addressed Clive brightly. 'Not sitting up today?' Clive was silent. She squeezed his hand but made no move to kiss him. 'Are you off bananas now?' she asked, noticing the bowl of uneaten fruit on the table. 'Oh, dear – I've brought some more.'

She searched for another conversational gambit. A blown-up photograph had been pinned to the wall beside the bed. It was Nell's gift: a view of the front of their house. 'Ah, you've got it pinned up! It does look effective, doesn't it? Nell's going to be delighted when I tell her. She sends her love, by the way – they both do—'

Irritated by her manner, Singleton broke in abruptly. 'We've hit a black spot, I'm afraid. It happens: the condition intensifies, or there's a reaction to the treatment. Sometimes it's psychological—'

'I wouldn't think it's that,' Ruth protested.

'—or a combination of all three.'

No one spoke; Clive remained motionless. Once again, Ruth plunged into the breach. 'I just met Becca Crichton, helping with the fête. She sends her regards.' Silence. 'Everyone's still asking about you, the phone never stops ringing.'

'He got a case of champagne this morning.' Singleton said.

'Oh?'

'From his company.'

'That was decent of them, wasn't it? Have you had some?' Clive looked away, mute. 'Is he allowed?' she asked Singleton. 'Why don't we all have some?'

'He's putting it in the auction at the fête.'

'Well,' Ruth said, forcing a smile, 'it's a good cause.'

'Is that a regular thing,' Singleton asked, 'sending champagne?'

Clive spoke at last, his voice barely audible. 'Only to has-beens.'

'Nonsense,' Ruth said, 'it's probably just my winning ways with the MD again . . .' She faltered; Clive rolled his eyes towards her in ironic disbelief. Every day, she thought, the distance between them grew more vast.

A nurse knocked on the door and entered; she wore a surgical mask and carried a tray of injection paraphernalia. 'Puncture time,' Singleton told Ruth. 'We're stepping them up for a few days. Nothing to worry about.'

'I'll wait outside,' Ruth said quickly.

'There's no need,' Singleton assured her. He offered her a mask from the nurse's tray. 'Here, take one of these—'

'No,' Ruth said, visibly frightened, 'really . . .'

'Have you got a thing about injections?' Singleton asked, curious.

'No,' Clive said bitterly. 'She's got a thing about my body.'

Ruth hastened out of the room. In the corridor, two young men were gazing out of a window at the fête. One of the men was in a wheelchair that was festooned with a cluster of red and yellow balloons. Ruth made her way to the other end of the corridor. In a moment, the consultant joined her.

'What's happening to him?' she asked, struggling to control her emotions.

Singleton shrugged. 'Bitterness. Guilt. Fear. The champagne was unfortunate; he thinks it means he's lost his job. Which would suggest that someone has informed the company.'

'No, surely not,' Ruth said firmly – and realised, even as she spoke, that it must be true. 'Not Bill!'

'You may have to revise your plans,' Singleton said.

'I've no plans,' she said, shaken. 'Except to get him home and look after him.'

'Until he dies. Which you hope he'll do painlessly and comparatively swiftly? Before anyone else knows the truth?'

The truth startled her, but she couldn't deny it. 'Yes,' she said defiantly.

'Supposing the truth gets out?'

She'd already worked that one out. 'I'll deny it.'

'That may not work,' Singleton warned her. 'Have you thought of an alternative?'

'There is no alternative. Not in our lives.'

Singleton saw the despair in her eyes, and softened. 'There's a young man down there, Morrie . . .' he nodded at the couple by the window. 'He's in the same condition as your husband. That's his lover with him. Let me introduce you—'

Ruth recoiled: 'No!'

'The lover's called Scott,' the consultant continued. 'He's kept his young man alive longer than anyone would've thought possible. Talk to them.'

'No!' she repeated. How could she explain that the mere sight of those . . . kind of people made her feel queasy? She tried to compose herself. 'I've led a very conventional life, Dr Singleton. You could call it sheltered. Or even respectable. There are some things I can't . . . experience.'

'Clive wasn't so sheltered,' Singleton said, not unkindly.

'I know that now,' she said, 'but . . .' her voice trailed off.

'But even he wouldn't want any truck with queers? Is that what you mean?'

Before she could answer, the nurse emerged from Clive's room and approached Ruth, saying,'I'm sorry, Mrs Gregory. Your husband says, will you excuse him? He wants to sleep after the injection.'

Ruth suppressed a flicker of anger and walked slowly towards the lift, Singleton beside her.

'You can't forgive him, can you?' the consultant asked.

How dare he? Ruth thought. 'It doesn't matter whether I forgive him or not. It doesn't even matter what I feel. What matters is how I behave. I have to protect my family. No one talks about "disgrace" these days, do

they? But it's still there. If I can just stay in control –
reasonably calm, reasonably supportive – until he dies,
that's all that matters.'

'I hope you manage it,' Singleton said. She caught his
sceptical expression, and stepped into the lift.

Chapter 5

'What's going on?' Bill Stanhope asked Geoff Harris. 'Paddy here said you had a pulled muscle.'

Paddy Firth had waylaid him at the entrance of Routh Electronics when he'd arrived at work, and taken him down to the company gym on what Stanhope now saw was a false alarm. Harris, his muscles clearly in fine form, was making use of a complicated system of weights. 'You said—' Stanhope began.

'We just wanted a word,' Harris said, 'and since you've been consistently unavailable for over a week, we thought a little ruse was in order.' He wound up his weights routine with a flourish. 'Look at that! Been testing my strength. To make sure I've still got some,' he added significantly.

Stanhope's discomfort was obvious. 'Look,' he said, 'I can't stay here. I've got work . . .'

Harris gently pushed him into a chair. 'We've all got work.' Firth sat beside him. 'How was the blood?' he asked.

'Blood?'

'Pretty thin stuff, mine must be,' said Harris. 'Spend too much time at high altitudes.'

'What's all this about?' Stanhope asked disingenuously, sensing a trap.

'I was called in for a medical last Thursday,' Firth said. 'My routine check-up wasn't due for two months.'

'I was called in last Wednesday,' said Harris. 'Six weeks early. And taking blood's a new thing, isn't it?'

'I told you,' Stanhope bluffed, perspiring. 'Administrative convenience. I'm establishing new guidelines.'

'Is that all?' Firth asked suspiciously.

Stanhope shrugged. 'Bit of a flap in the company, in case you lot are overworked.'

'Balls!' Harris said; 'You mean because of Clive?'

'Indirectly.'

'Clive wasn't overworked,' Firth said. 'He loved it. Cancer's just one of those things, right? Nothing to do with overwork. Poor bugger. How is he, anyway?'

'Ah ... hopeful of a remission, I believe. Quite hopeful.'

'He'll be back at work, then?' Harris asked.

'Possibly.'

'Someone said he'd had the champagne,' Firth said, fishing.

'Listen, Bill,' Harris said, leaning in close. 'Five members of the senior management team have been tested so far. The only operation we all pulled together was the big one in the States, back end of '84.'

'So?' Stanhope asked, on the edge of panic.

Firth eyed him narrowly. 'We were at the Boden plant, briefly. Waltram, upstate New York.' He waited for Stanhope's reaction and saw that the doctor was genuinely nonplussed.

'Come on, Bill,' Harris coaxed. 'The Boden plant's under observation now, for not doing a radioactive springclean.'

'No, no, no ...' In his surge of relief, Stanhope dropped his guard. 'You're barking up the wrong tree there.' The two men watched him uncertainly. 'Your blood's fine, by the way – nothing but pure vodka, both of you.'

Harris continued to watch him carefully. 'Good. Sorry about all this, Bill. Only, you know how it is – rub shoulders with someone who's bad news and before you know where you are, you're fighting for video nasties with the other unemployables.'

Stanhope stood up. 'I've got to go.'

'See you on the third?' Firth asked. The doctor looked blank. 'Ruth and Clive's knees-up, isn't it? She seems hell-bent on going through with it.'

'We're not invited. We're hardly close friends, you know.'

'It's duty for us, really,' Harris said. 'Merry-making. Christ!'

'Cheers,' Stanhope said hastily, and started out of the gym. Behind him, he heard Firth ask, 'Which tree *do* we bark up, then?' Pretending not to have heard, he kept on walking.

While Stanhope tried to escape his interrogators at Routh Electronics, his daughter waited nervously outside the Langley election office for Clive's son, rehearsing what she'd come to tell him. Martin finally emerged, laden with leaflets, and headed for his car, pointedly ignoring Sharon until she called his name. 'Sorry,' he replied, briskly stowing the leaflets into his car, 'I've got another helper.'

'I haven't come about the campaign,' Sharon said.

'Good. You're a week behind on tactics.'

'I know you phoned . . .' she began.

'Really?' She'd expected him to be angry about her having avoided his calls, but she hadn't expected this glacial chill.

'How're things?' she asked, trying to regain her balance.

He shrugged. 'Averagely terrible. If you mean my father, he's coming out soon.'

'I'm glad.'

'He's not much better.'

'I'm sorry.' He looked so tired and drawn, her heart

went out to him. 'Listen . . . I wanted to tell you that I'm going to Switzerland . . .'

'I don't care if you're going to the Labour committee rooms,' he said cuttingly.

'I've got to. They're making me.' In spite of herself she started to cry.

Martin looked at her curiously. 'Making you?'

'Mummy and Daddy . . .'

He walked round to her side of the car and put a tentative arm around her. 'I thought we had something going,' he said softly.

'We did. It's not my fault.'

'What is it, then?'

'I don't know. They frightened me – they said I had to be out of the way.'

'Out of the way of *what*?'

'It's your father,' she said tearfully.

'Sharon,' he said, bewildered, 'I've got enough to deal with at the moment—'

'I shouldn't be here.' She backed away from him. 'I just wanted you to understand . . . It's something worse . . . Much worse.' He reached for her again but she turned and ran from him, as though from . . . from some dread disease, he thought. Perturbed and perplexed, he watched her go.

A week later, Becca Crichton waited anxiously outside the door behind which the golf club women's committee was deciding her fate. She looked far more composed than she felt, listening to the murmur of the indistinguishable voices. Never religious, she prayed now for the strength to accept still another rejection, if that was how it turned out. She was lighting a cigarette when she heard footsteps down the passage-way; Ruth hurried into view.

'You made it!' said Becca, delighted.

'How far have they gone?' Ruth asked.

'Too far, probably. It was good of you to come,' Becca said fervently.

'I have to do the routine things.'

Becca nodded empathetically. 'Please,' she said as Ruth moved towards the closed door, 'tell the dragon ladies that golf's my only healthy activity, will you? I need it on medical grounds. And if I've made a pass at any of their husbands, to take it as a comment on their good taste. And—'

Already guiltily late, Ruth could delay no longer. She patted Becca's hand and opened the door, through which Becca saw the six other committee members look up with some surprise.

As she seated herself at the table, Ruth acknowledged the women's welcoming smiles. 'Sorry I'm late,' she apologised.

'Not at all, Ruth.' Madge Pearson, who was chairing the meeting, felt that a speech might be in order. 'I'm sure we're all delighted to see you. May I say on behalf of everyone—'

'No, please,' Ruth protested, 'don't let me interrupt.'

'Well,' Madge said, 'Annie has the floor.'

'I was simply saying,' Annie addressed the group, 'that if you break the rules, you pay the price. It's as simple as that to me. Offenders shouldn't go unpunished, in this club or anywhere else. There's too much letting people off these days—'

'I agree,' Eleanor Holmes interjected.

'—and I don't want anyone to think this is some kind of revenge. She can insult me until she's blue in the face, quite frankly, but the rule book clearly states that any member conducting him or herself improperly—'

'Yes, thank you, Annie,' Madge said impatiently. 'We know what the rule book states. Some of us have been here long enough to remember the rule book being revised – and long enough to remember what Becca was like at her best, and to hope that all this is temporary. Becca's a brilliant player, remember.' She handed a letter across the table to Ruth. 'We've had this fairly contrite letter from Becca, promising good behaviour. Quite amusing, really. There's been some argument about how we should respond.'

Ruth glanced at the opening paragraph: *I know I've offended – more than once – and I'm sorry. I'll steer clear of the Remy Martin and of the male members – on the premises, that is – but please don't throw me out of the club.* Ruth looked up at Madge. 'I think we should give her a chance. Don't you?'

'I don't accept,' Annie said, unbending. 'I'm sorry, but I don't think that letter's amusing. I think it's quite offensive. Patronising. "I'll do detention on the eighth green, tied to a flagpole if you like." She's laughing at us.'

'It's her style, isn't it?' Ruth said.

'Personally, I don't buy all that,' Eleanor said righteously.

'There's no doubt that she can be a pain in the neck,' Madge conceded, 'but—'

'More than a pain in the neck,' Ginnie Bradshaw broke in, her opposition a surprise to Madge and Ruth.

'She took Irene Doran's husband, after all,' said Pat Wood, always easily swayed.

'That's really no concern of ours,' Madge pointed out.

'She's a disruptive drunk,' Ginnie blurted out. 'She should go.'

Ruth felt a surge of loyalty toward Becca. 'That'd be a pity,' she said.

'Hear, hear!' said Pamela Greenfield, declaring herself.

'After all,' Ruth said, 'she is taking steps to improve.'

'Who says?' Annie asked with hostility.

'I happen to know.'

Madge glanced round at her fellow judges. 'It's distasteful, this, isn't it?'

'That's what we're here for,' Ginnie said.

Ruth poured herself a glass of water from the carafe on the table and drained it, trying to frame an acceptable proposal. 'How long has it been since the last incident?' she asked Madge.

'A couple of months.'

'Why not say if she stays quiet until the end of the year,' Ruth suggested, 'she can renew her membership like everyone else. If not, we'll have to take another look.'

'That seems reasonable,' Madge said, relieved.

'Sorry,' said Annie. 'I've got to say that it doesn't seem reasonable to me. The fact is, we're members of this club because it's the best in the area. It *won't* be the best if we condone the wrong kind of behaviour. People will go elsewhere. I happen to believe that people must take the consequences of their actions.'

'Me, too,' Eleanor chimed in.

'Becca *lives* with the consequences of her actions,' Ruth said, 'rather unhappily.'

'We all have problems,' Annie sneered.

'Do we?' Ruth asked quietly.

'Well, you certainly have, Ruth,' Annie said deliberately, 'and I can't think what it is about you that makes you so eager to defend, well, loose living, or whatever you want to call it.'

The knot in Ruth's stomach tightened. 'Loose living?'

'I must ask you to speak through the chair,' Madge told Annie sternly, 'and to withdraw that last remark.'

Annie lowered her eyes. 'Sorry. But that *is* what we're talking about, isn't it?' No one responded. 'I withdraw.'

'Well,' Madge said briskly, 'I didn't want to put it to the vote, but if there are strong feelings, it looks as though I'll have to. *For* Becca?' She looked round questioningly. Still reeling from Annie's remark, Ruth raised her hand mechanically. Pamela Greenwood and Pat Wood followed suit.

'Against?' Annie, Eleanor and Ginnie raised their hands. Madge looked at Ruth and sighed. 'I'll throw mine in with you, Ruth. Someone tell Becca she's off the hook.'

Annie shot Ruth a furious look, then turned her attention to Ginnie, who absently reached for the carafe of water and began to refill the glass Ruth had used. 'That was Ruth's glass,' Annie blurted out.

'Oh, was it?' Ginnie asked innocently. 'Well, I don't suppose it matters.'

'It's best to be sure.' Annie handed her an unused glass, then picked up the first glass and started toward the door. No one noticed her action except Ruth, who went cold with horror.

Ruth stood up, made her way past a jubilant Becca and moved like an automaton towards the entrance hall. Wordlessly she passed Annie, ostentatiously conversing with two of her cronies. On the far side of the evening crowd of club members, Geoff Harris raised a hand in greeting and turned into the bar. Disoriented, she nearly collided with Bill Stanhope, who mumbled 'Sorry' and hurried past her. Dazed, with the noise pressing in on her ears, the lights misting before her eyes, she made her way out of the club.

Chapter 6

Ruth filled the next three weeks with ceaseless activity; combined with the Valium, it kept reality at bay. With Mrs Gordon's help, she saw to it that the house was spotless when Singleton released Clive, as promised, from hospital. He was much improved, although terribly tired, and spent most of his time in his room poring over business papers. Ruth kept herself occupied with preparations for the party. She sent invitations to fifty couples and figured, based on past experience, that about eighty people would show up. She booked a five-piece band, hired fairy lights for the garden, and arranged for huge amounts of elaborate food. She ordered cases of champagne, and a cake decorated with a glittering silver '25'. With uncharacteristic extravagance, she splurged on matching silk party dresses for herself and Nell.

She wasn't surprised when ten couples declined – that was the normal ratio – and when most of the others didn't respond at all, she told Nell it didn't mean they weren't coming, only that people didn't pay much attention to the old-fashioned social graces these days. But at eleven o'clock on the night, only thirteen people, including four neighbours and the vicar and his wife, milled forlornly around the sparkling house and garden. Despite all Ruth's efforts, the occasion seemed more like a wake than a party.

Clive watched the proceedings bleakly, taking no part. While Nell danced sedately with a man three times her age, Ruth urged the vicar to have some more cake. Out of the corner of her eye, she saw her husband leave the room; she excused herself and followed him into the hall. 'Where are you going?' she asked sharply.

'To bed.' Wearily, Clive started to climb the stairs.

'We have guests,' Ruth said, tight-lipped.

Clive laughed bitterly. 'Really? I'd scarcely noticed.'

'It doesn't matter,' Ruth protested.

'Give it a rest, Ruth,' he implored. 'They *know*. The ones who didn't come – they know! The company, the golf club, they *know*!' She shook her head, denying the unthinkable. Clive lowered his voice: 'And Martin.'

Ruth could see her son in the drawing room, making a valiant effort to engage the vicar in conversation. 'No,' she said stricken. 'Not Martin.'

'Yes! He can't even look at me. He hardly comes home.'

'He was offered a room near his headquarters!'

'He *knows*!'

Ruth paused, then spoke in a fierce whisper: 'You have to go through with this, Clive!'

'Make my excuses. Say I'm exhausted.' He started up the stairs. She followed and grabbed his arm.

'No! You owe it to me and to the children!'

'But especially to you,' Clive said, his voice heavy with defeat. 'It's over,' he said, 'isn't it?'

Ruth faltered. 'Don't let's . . . Not now . . . Give me time. I haven't worked it out yet, even how I feel about your being unfaithful.'

'Unfaithful?' He stared at her in disbelief. 'I've never been unfaithful to you in my life! I poked a dirty little tart when I was too pissed to show good judgement. And now I'm paying for it.'

Involuntarily, Ruth blurted out the question that had tormented her for weeks. 'Had you done it before?'

'What?' Clive asked, dismayed. 'Jesus—'

'Had you?'

'It's not important,' Clive hedged. 'I spent a lot of time away from home . . .'

In spite of everything, she'd been unprepared for the answer that was written on his face. 'You had!' she said, incredulous. 'Hadn't you?'

He struggled for words. 'I said it's not important . . . I thought you probably guessed.'

Anger pushed past her control: '*Were they all girls?*' He looked at her blankly. Before he could respond, the doorbell rang. Blindly, Ruth went to answer it.

Becca Crichton stood on the doorstep, resplendent in gold brocade, bedecked with jewellery, red hair loose round her shoulders, arms filled with a huge bouquet of white roses. Seeing Ruth's face, she hesitated. 'Sorry,' she said, 'it's the Wicked Fairy.' Ruth couldn't speak; she took the flowers and stepped back. 'I know it's invitation only,' Becca said, 'but some of those who had them didn't deserve them.'

'You're welcome,' Ruth said, straining to recover her composure. 'Come in, please . . .'

Becca stepped inside. 'I rounded up a few other unin-vited well-wishers,' she grinned. 'They'll clear the food, if nothing else.' She waved through the open front door, signalling through the darkness. Confidentially, in a voice too low for Clive to hear, she said, 'There's talk in these parts. I don't want to listen, but it's coming up through the drains now. If there's anyone you'd rather didn't hear it that way, tell them yourselves. Soon.' Her friends, three men and two women, came through the door behind her and, with a casual wave at the host and hostess, made straight for the food and drink. Becca grabbed the last man by the sleeve and pushed him towards Ruth. 'This is Dennis.'

The tall, sandy-haired, angular man spoke in a rough Glaswegian accent. 'How're you doing?' he asked amiably.

48

'You should talk to Dennis,' Becca said significantly. 'You've got something in common.'

'Hello,' Ruth said politely. Without warning, her emotional barricades crumbled and tears streamed down her cheeks; she turned away.

Undaunted, Becca plunged ahead: 'Oh, he's not that bad,' she laughed, 'though I did warn you about that shirt,' she chided Dennis. 'What're you doing up there, Clive?' she asked her host, who stood uncertainly halfway up the stairs. 'Being a social outcast? Come on down and meet another one.'

With a faint smile, he complied. 'Hello, Becca.' She met him at the bottom of the stairs. Quite deliberately, she put her arms around him and kissed him on the mouth.

'How're you doing?' she asked.

'Bloody awful.' For the first time all evening, Clive relaxed.

'Come on,' Becca said, leading the way into the drawing room. Ruth and Clive watched from the doorway as, almost miraculously, her energy and good humour cleared the air. The mood visibly lifted and a babble of voices broke out, with Becca's rising above the others. 'You weren't leaving, were you, Vicar? Not before we've danced, surely. Don't I recall a fevered Bossa Nova? . . . Is this Martin? . . . It can't be! . . . Sorry, Vicar, you're demoted to second dance . . . What marvellous food! This Pavlova won't stay unraped for long . . . Can one get a drink around here? I'll regret champagne, but what's another regret, more or less? Have we missed the toast? . . . Oh, come on, we must have a toast! Has no one proposed—? Well, I will, then. Listen, everyone – a toast!' The guests fell silent; Becca raised a glass. Ruth smiled; Clive took her hand in both of his, and kissed it.

'Ruth and Clive,' Becca proclaimed. The guests picked up her enthusiasm, lifted their glasses and came in on cue.

'Ruth and Clive!'

49

Chapter 7

The morning after the party Ruth felt that the air between herself and Clive had cleared to some extent. Perhaps now they could communicate; perhaps the tension in the house would ease. Uppermost in her mind, though, was Becca's advice: 'Tell them yourself,' she'd said. If Martin did know, what exactly had he heard, and where? And what, if anything, might he have said to Nell?

Ruth found her daughter on the patio, collecting the last traces of debris. She steeled herself and said, with great trepidation, 'Can we talk?'

The girl put down the tray of dirty glasses she was carrying. 'About Dad, you mean?' Ruth nodded. With more poise than Ruth could have imagined, Nell put a reassuring arm around her mother and said, 'Don't worry about me, Mum. Martin and I spoke to Dad last night, after you went to bed. We'd heard . . . things. We had to find out if they were true.'

Ruth stared at her daughter, amazed at the role reversal: Nell was trying to protect *her*. A wave of mixed emotions swept over her: love, relief, humility. Nell hugged her. 'We'll manage,' she said. 'It's not the end of the world, you know.' Ruth nodded mutely.

It struck Ruth later that both her children possessed a degree of sexual sophistication that probably exceeded her own. How could it be otherwise, with obscene words and unnatural acts turning up as everyday fare in newspapers, films and pop songs? It would have been unrealistic to expect the children to make the effort she herself made to avoid that kind of trash. Now, despite her fierce instinct to protect them, she was glad they'd been spared the ignorance that had made her so vulnerable.

She had never allowed herself to consider whether or not Nell was still a virgin, although she had no reason to believe otherwise. Martin, she knew, was 'sexually active', a term she found trivialising and offensive. Didn't people make love any more? Did they merely 'have sex', indulging their animal urges? Sharon wasn't the only girl Martin had brought home with him. The first time he'd done it, Ruth had been outraged. Clive had given her a little lecture about changing morals: 'If they don't do it here, they'll only do it somewhere else.' They had argued about it at some length; she didn't want Martin – or, even more, Nell – to think she condoned what she knew to be wrong. Eventually, Clive had made her feel so foolish and old-fashioned that she'd relented. In retrospect, she thought he'd seemed proud of the evidence of his son's virility.

She saw little of Martin as the by-election campaign neared its climax, but on election day he phoned, greatly excited, to invite the whole family to the election night ceremonies. Ruth was delighted; she could tell that Clive, although he said little, was pleased as well. With Nell, they arrived at the entrance to the community hall just as the returning officer was stentorially announcing the results. 'I, Joseph Thomas Brady,' he intoned, 'returning officer for the constituency of Berkshire West, declare that the total number of votes cast in this by-election was twenty-one thousand, nine hundred and eighty-five. The votes cast for each candidate were as follows: Arthur George Blackmore, two thousand, one hundred and fourteen votes; David Curzon Langley, twelve thousand, six hundred and eighty-three votes.' They could hear cheers and applause from the audience inside. 'John Whitaker, seven thousand, one hundred and eighty-six votes.'

At the door, Clive faltered. 'Is this going to be all right?' he asked Ruth.

'He invited us!'

Nell grinned. 'Don't let's stay long. I have my image to consider.'

Inside, the voice droned on to its official conclusion. 'I hereby declare David Curzon Langley the elected member of parliament for this constituency.'

Amidst the applause, Ruth and Clive made their way through cheering blue-rosetted supporters to the back of the hall, where they stood unobtrusively. Martin emerged from the crowd and made his way towards them. 'You made it! Good!'

Clive shook his son's hand. 'Well done, Martin!'

'Thanks. I feel as if I'd won the seat myself.'

'You practically did,' Ruth said.

'What a majority!' Clive enthused. 'Must be twenty percent up!'

'Yes. SDP were nowhere on tactics, thank God.'

Nell felt compelled to declare herself. 'Where can I make a contribution to the Labour man's deposit?'

'Don't worry,' Martin told her. 'The IRA are paying.' Hearing his name called, he shot a victory salute in the direction of someone in the crowd.

'Go and join the celebrations,' Clive said warmly. 'We're off. Just wanted to be in at the kill. It's a bit of excitement.' He punched Martin's arm proudly.

'We won't expect you home tonight,' Ruth said. She kissed her son affectionately and turned to leave with Clive when a rather portly, balding man, flushed with victory, appeared beside Martin and grabbed his arm.

'Ah, now this is the lad!' said the new MP.

'Terrific, David,' Martin said. 'Congratulations. Great show.'

'No, great show *you*!' Langley insisted. His eye lit on Martin's family, who were trying to move away through the crush of the crowd. 'Your parents?' he asked. 'Can't be, they look so young.'

Nervously, Martin fumbled at introductions. 'Yes, er . . . David Langley . . . MP . . .'

'Mr and Mrs Gregory,' Langley said, shaking their hands vigorously. 'Very nice of you to cross the constituency boundary.'

'And my sister, Nell.'

Langley looked her up and down, then winked at Martin. 'We could've used her on the hustings, surely?'

'Only as target practice,' Nell parried.

'The campaign's meant so much to Martin,' Ruth injected hastily.

'He's meant so much to the campaign. He's going places, this one, you know. A few years and this'll be *his* scene. You'll be cheering him then, all of you.' Heedless of the poignancy of his remark, Langley continued, 'If you can hang around for the next few weeks, Martin, there's plenty of good will stuff to be done.'

'Oh, I can hang around, thanks.'

Langley grinned. 'Good. Observe me kiss a few carnival queens, dole out some prizes—'

'And work on the maiden speech at the same time. I get the picture.'

Langley addressed all four Gregorys expansively. 'They'll be opening the fizzy white stuff at headquarters now. Why don't you come over and join us?'

Martin's discomfort was obvious to Langley. 'Er . . . my father hasn't been very well lately. They were just leaving . . .'

'Ah,' said Langley, 'I'm sorry to hear that. Well, some other time.' His attention already elsewhere, he moved away.

Avoiding his parents' eyes, Martin tried vainly to recoup the situation. 'There might be some people over there you wouldn't want to meet,' he said lamely.

'I know *I* wouldn't,' Nell said pointedly. 'I can't afford the risk of contamination.'

Her words were almost drowned out by the strains of *Rule Britannia*. 'Well,' Martin said awkwardly, 'goodnight, then.' Mortified, Clive started towards the door, with Ruth and Nell behind him. Martin caught at his sister's arm. 'Couldn't you have stopped him?'

'He's not been out for a week,' Nell said reproachfully. 'And you asked them.'

Martin looked away, shamefaced. 'I didn't think they'd accept.'

Nell hurried after her parents. 'Martin will make a wonderful MP,' she said, catching up. 'Only there's no shire sodden enough to hold him. What did he think you were going to do, Dad? Dominate the back benches?'

'I suppose he was afraid there'd be someone there who'd heard gossip,' Ruth said as they reached the car.

'Well, I'm sorry,' Nell said impulsively, 'but it does seem like a cue for my own well-aimed kick in the teeth. I mean, you may as well have them all in one go.' Clive and Ruth looked at her, mystified. 'The fact is, not only am I not going to re-sit A-levels, I'm not actually going back to school, either.' She climbed quickly into the back seat.

'Wait a minute—' Clive began.

'Let's go home,' Ruth said. She opened Clive's door, then went round and got behind the wheel, started the car up and manoeuvred it onto the road.

Having taken the plunge, Nell continued. 'Can you imagine what the Upper Sixth might do with an AIDS scare? It'd be surgical masks with designer labels. In no time. I've found a photographer – he's called Nicky Harding. He'll let me set up for him and help with his printing.'

'What kind of photographer?' Clive asked, turning to look at her.

'Somewhere between soft porn and the *National*

Geographic,' Nell said, feigning casualness. 'Does it matter?'

'Yes,' Clive said disapprovingly.

'He'll pay me. I'll work quite long hours but I'll come home at night and be around if you need me. Not like Martin. I expect it'll be awful, but not as awful as trying to knock off French and German while my friends swig Dettol and stay downwind of me.' Ruth tightened her grip on the wheel.

'You could go away,' Clive said, concealing the anguish he was feeling. 'You could go to a college, perhaps, or a crammer's—'

'Sorry.'

'Listen,' Clive said forcefully, 'I want to see your future taken care of while I've still got some life in me!'

Nell's face was barely distinguishable in the darkness, but her words were clear and deliberate. 'My future's been no business of yours since you did whatever it was you did.'

Ruth swerved to avoid an oncoming car, and tried to concentrate on her driving. Clive gasped, then stared despairingly into the darkness, saying nothing until Ruth pulled the car into their drive. Demoralised, he followed Ruth towards the house while Nell ran ahead to unlock the front door. 'I knew I shouldn't have told them,' he muttered.

'Don't be silly, Dad,' Nell shot back over her shoulder. 'I'd heard it in Sainsbury's before I heard it from you.' She opened the door; a bunch of keys and an envelope lay just inside, beneath the letter box. Ruth picked them up, opened the envelope and scanned the contents. *It's too much*, she thought; *I can't take any more.* Clive and Nell looked on, baffled, as she ripped the note into shreds. 'Mrs Gordon . . .' she said helplessly.

Chapter 8

When Becca Crichton learned that Ruth had been given some transparent excuse about conflicting schedules at the charity shop and asked to discontinue her work there, she was shocked but not surprised; sanctimonious hypocrisy was nothing new to her. She rang Ruth immediately. 'If you're free tomorrow afternoon,' she said, knowing that would have been Ruth's Oxfam day, 'come along with me. There's this new planet I've discovered . . .'

Ruth's first thought on entering the hotel ballroom was that the clothes, the music and the people all seemed to belong to a gentler time, long out of fashion. The room itself, with its spacious gallery and crystal chandelier, must have been quite smart in its day. Now, its faded gentility suited the couples, middle-aged and older, who danced with earnest concentration to the strains of 'Alice Blue Gown,' played only slightly too sweetly by six bored musicians. Some of the women had a dowdy dignity; others defied the passing years in flamboyant prints. Were they there for the dancing, Ruth wondered, or because they had nothing else to do?

She followed Becca, who made her way between tables around which people sat, sipping tea. Becca stopped beside a large potted plant. 'The child's called Fraser,' she said, indicating a boy of about ten who sat at a table in the corner, eating ice cream. Beside him was one of the men Becca had brought to the anniversary party. 'He's Dennis's son. Fraser's a haemophiliac. He got AIDS from a contaminated blood transfusion. He was nursed on his own in the children's ward. I found him trying to get down the fire escape one day. We seemed to have something to offer each other.'

Ruth looked around, amazed. 'And you meet here?'

'We don't "meet". They just come here on Dennis's half-day. With the other refugees. Come on,' she said encouragingly. Dennis looked up when they reached his table, but remained seated. 'Hello, Dennis. Remember Ruth? I took you to her party but you got culture shock from her French windows.'

Dennis appraised Ruth with shrewd blue eyes. 'I remember. Hi.'

'Hello.' Ruth had forgotten his Glaswegian accent.

The boy looked up; his pale, pinched face piercingly reminded Ruth of Clive. 'This is Fraser,' Becca said, ruffling his hair affectionately. The two women sat down.

'Your partner's been agitating,' Dennis told Becca. 'He was afraid you wouldn't make it for the Latin-American.'

Becca looked across to where a dapper gentleman in a bow tie was adroitly leading a woman through the steps of a St Bernard's waltz. 'As if I'd let him down. This is my spiritual home. Specially since I stopped drinking with the grown-ups.' She turned to Ruth. 'How does it square with the charity shop?'

'It's livelier,' Ruth said, bemused.

'What did Clive say when you got the push?' Becca asked, curious.

'I haven't told him.'

'But you worked there two days a week . . .'

'He thinks I still do. I need two days away from him,' she confessed.

'I thought you were talking.'

'It didn't last.'

The St Bernard's waltz came to an end amidst graceful swirls and dips. A waitress set a tea service on their table.

Becca turned to Dennis: 'Ruth has also been relieved of her place on the golf club committee. "Pro tem".'

'Oh, aye,' Dennis said wryly.

'Dennis thinks the golf course should be a leisure centre for the unwaged,' Becca said. A thought struck her: 'I'm unwaged!'

'You're a fucking parasite,' Dennis said irritated. 'And the golf club's an affront to democracy.'

Ruth looked around, embarrassed. The strains of a rumba began and the bow-tied dancer presented himself to Becca. 'May I?' he asked. Close up, Ruth saw that he was at least twenty-five years Becca's senior; his neat moustache and sideburns were white, and his brown hair was clearly off the peg.

'You certainly may, Edgar,' Becca said, rising. 'How splendid you look today. She glanced at his hairpiece; 'And how youthful!'

As Edgar drew Becca towards the dance floor, Dennis and Ruth heard him ask, 'Is that your lady friend? She's on Valium, isn't she?' Becca laughed, but her reply was lost as they danced out of earshot.

Ruth laughed as well, nervously. 'I am, as a matter of fact. How did he know?'

Dennis shrugged, as uncomfortable with Ruth as she was with him. She looked around again, surveying the scene.

'This is a new departure for me . . .'

'Oh, aye . . . ?' Dennis said, prickly. In the awkward silence that followed, Ruth unconsciously reverted to her customary hostessy manner. 'What do you do?' she asked politely.

'Do?'

'I mean, where do you work?'

'Carpet warehouse.'

'Is it interesting?'

Dennis snorted with amusement. 'Is it *what*?' Becca

and Dennis swept past, rumba-ing madly. 'What's *she* on?' Dennis asked, waving at Becca. 'She keeps coming round Fraser like it was Christmas. She lose her own kids?'

'Her husband got custody and took them to America.' Dennis shrugged and made no effort to continue the conversation. Ruth tried again. 'Are you married?'

'I don't know,' Dennis said cryptically. 'The wife went out the door one night five years ago and never came back. Couldn't take it when we found out about him. Or perhaps she just couldn't get her tongue round "haemophilia".'

Ruth ignored the sarcasm. 'And when did you find out that he had the virus, as well?'

'Eighteen months. I thought God was piling it on a bit there.'

'Though if he's only a carrier . . .'

'I know,' Dennis sighed. He'd heard it before. 'I know. He could live forever. Or he could get a bout of flu that went wrong and it'd be cheerio.'

'Did you leave Glasgow because you were ostracised?' Ruth's interest was genuine enough, but her propriety put Dennis' back up.

'No, they don't do much of that in tenements,' he said. 'It's more like pissing on the doormat and shoving not very nice things through the letter box. Till you start running.'

His rudeness jolted her into an admission: 'I wanted to run when I heard about Clive,' she confessed.

'You stuck to him, though, eh?' He smirked. 'And his big house, and his BMW?' He stood up. 'Want to dance?'

Speechless, Ruth followed him onto the dance floor where to her surprise, she began to relax. She saw Becca return to the table and begin an animated conversation with Fraser. 'Shouldn't he be at school?' she asked Dennis.

'Think this is a bit unwholesome for him?'

'No,' she lied, tensing again.

'Wouldn't have done for *your* kids, though, would it?' Clearly enjoying her discomfort, he skilfully negotiated a corner. 'He's still convalescing from his last fall. He'll go to school when I can find one he won't be thrown out of.'

'Excuse me,' Edgar said, cutting in. 'May I?' Ruth protested but then, observing the habit of a lifetime, fell compliantly into step. 'I haven't observed you here before,' Edgar said in gentrified North Country tones. The Latin American section ended and with scarcely a pause, a foxtrot began.

'No,' Ruth replied, 'It's my first time.' Decisively, Edgar led her into the new dance. 'You should come regular; you'd never need tranquillisers. It removed the trauma from my retirement.'

'Really?' Ruth said politely.

'Oh, yes. And if you don't mind me saying so, you'd manage your reverse turns a lot better.'

'I haven't danced like this for years,' Ruth said shyly.

'You're quite good. Though I'd say your friend's got the edge. She's improved, of course, since she's been off the drink. I've told her . . .'

He took her into a slightly adventurous spin. Becca, watching from her seat, turned to Dennis. 'I think I may actually have done something right for a change,' she said.

Clive's strength returned gradually and, with it, a forced, almost manic optimism. He clung to the hope of returning to work; however badly he'd failed as a husband and father, his value as an employee was beyond question. He had more contributions to make, and he was determined to make them. Work was what gave his life meaning; without it, he thought, he might as well be dead already. Obsessively, he plotted his tactics.

The first step was to see Singleton alone and get his approval. During Clive's next examination, the consultant remarked on Ruth's absence. 'I've decided I'm a big boy now,' Clive replied. 'She's waiting downstairs.'

'You can tell her you're doing well. It's not unusual at this stage. Your blood count's stable.'

'How about signing me off?' Clive asked hopefully.

'Gladly. You'll need regular checks, of course.'

'No problem. I can go back to work then?'

'As far as I'm concerned, there's no reason why you shouldn't.'

Clive was elated. 'And what was it you cooked up with the GP for the medical certificate?'

'Malignant fibrous growths in the lungs. It wasn't cooked up. It's the truth.'

'Good. That'll be my line, then. I really am feeling a hundred per cent better, you know.'

The consultant observed him shrewdly. 'I'm delighted.'

'Frankly,' Clive said confidentally, 'I think a good deal of this is mind over matter, don't you?'

'No,' Singleton said emphatically, 'I don't. In fact, we have a name for that attitude. We call it denial.'

'I can't think what I'm denying,' Clive said defiantly.

Singleton sighed. 'Have it your way. That's all, then. Unless you've any questions.'

Clive hesitated. 'As a matter of fact, there is something.'

'Yes?'

Clive tried to sound casual; he'd rehearsed this question, preparing himself. 'How will I know . . . when the next stage has started? If it ever does?'

'Is there any point in talking about it now?' the consultant asked.

Clive braced himself. 'Yes. I want to know.'

Singleton spoke clinically, but not unkindly. 'There could be sudden severe incontinence. Or paralysis,

61

perhaps – the seizing-up of a limb. Loss of balance, vomiting, tremor . . .'

'Thanks,' Clive said impassively.

'If you're contemplating anything drastic,' Singleton said quickly, 'I hope you'll talk to me first.'

'Don't worry. I'm worth more to my family alive than dead, at the moment. I expect my company will check with you when I tell them I'm ready to go back to work.'

'I wish someone here would offer *me* early retirement on full pay,' Singleton said. Clive thought he sounded wistful.

'I suppose this kind of work is depressing.'

'Lack of funds is depressing. Lack of cooperation, lack of understanding. Have you seen this?' He picked up a newspaper from his desk and held it out towards Clive, who glanced at the headline: COURTROOM CLEARED FOR POP STAR AIDS INQUEST.

'No,' Clive said evenly, 'and I don't want to.' His mission accomplished, he turned and walked resolutely out of the examining room.

Waiting for Clive, Ruth strolled aimlessly along the footpaths in the spacious hospital grounds. Once, twice, three times, two men in blue track suits jogged past her – one of them about Martin's age, lanky with long auburn hair, the other about ten years older, short and compact with a neat crew cut. As they came round for the fourth time, the older man slowed to a halt near Ruth, leaving his partner to continue on his own. 'That's five,' he called after the departing runner. 'Seven more, keep going . . . Nice pace, steady . . .' He gave Ruth a friendly nod. 'How's things?'

Surprised, she realised that the runner was Morrie, the AIDS patient Singleton had pointed out to her on the day of the fête, and the man beside her was his . . . Scott. She'd often seen them around the ward, Scott pushing

Morrie in his wheelchair. Scott looked at her quizzically, through intense blue eyes. 'Your husband, is it? In there with Dr Sin? Doctor Sins-of-the-Flesh, we call him.'

'Yes,' she said uneasily.

'We're next. I just want him to get this in first.'

'That's remarkable,' Ruth said. 'He was in a wheelchair . . . !'

'Yeah,' Scott said proudly. 'Wouldn't have given two pence for him a couple of months ago, eh? I couldn't stand watching him sit around and rot. Exercise is supposed to strengthen the immune system, whatever that means.'

'He's very young.'

'Twenty. Boredom's his trouble, so I shove in a bit of everything – astrology, herbal medicine . . . Unfortunately, we just got banned from the running track. Someone shopped him.'

'Shopped him?'

'Yeah. A health hazard in the showers, not that he ever used them. We're getting used to that kind of thing. Aren't you?'

Ruth warmed to his openness; 'I'm sorry,' she said sincerely.

'Oh, we'll find somewhere else,' Scott said. 'He's alive, that's the main thing, isn't it? As long as you keep them alive. That's nice,' he shouted as Morrie trotted past them. 'I'd been hoping to get him into a special race – it's called a "Joy Race" – but I'm not sure now he could manage it.'

'What's the distance?'

'Ten miles. He doesn't feel ill, you see, but he's got some new swellings. Doesn't your bloke have them?'

'It's just been his lungs so far.'

'It bloody knocks his morale, I can tell you. Anyway, it was always touch and go. Talk about races – people'd run bloody miles from *him* if they realised. We'd've had to keep him well covered.'

Touched by Scott's concern for his . . . friend, Ruth had a thought: 'Would it help if he was sponsored?'

'Who'd sponsor *him*?' Scott asked dismissively.

'I could canvass some people.'

Scott looked at her searchingly. 'You could?'

'Yes. I've done charity work.'

'People who'd keep quiet?'

'They wouldn't need to, particularly. He's just an individual, testing himself in a race, for charity.'

Scott shook his head. 'But he couldn't run for AIDS, could he?'

'No.' Ruth's gaze drifted back to the footpath; a boy of about Fraser's age rode past on a bike. She had a brainwave: 'He could run for haemophilia!'

'Yeah!' Scott said, brightening. 'He could, couldn't he? Might give him a bit of encouragement.' He considered Ruth carefully; for such an unlikely ally, she seemed quite genuine. 'I'd have to pick my moment to ask him, though. His moods! He's been *La Traviata* for days.' He spotted Clive walking towards them. 'Er . . . do we bring your bloke in on this?'

Ruth followed his gaze. 'No.'

Morrie ran past them again, and Scott took off in pursuit. 'Pick up your bloody feet, will you?' he shouted cheerfully. 'You just turned professional!'

Ruth hastened to join Clive, who watched the two runners with distaste. 'Devoted couple, aren't they? I used to hear them from my room, giggling in the corridor.'

'What did the doctor say?' Ruth asked anxiously.

'I'm well,' Clive said curtly. 'He says I'm well.'

'But Clive—'

'No negatives!' He turned to her accusingly: 'Don't you *want* me to get my job back? Do you want me filing recipes and sorting seed catalogues for the rest of my life?'

'The company won't have you!'

They had reached the car. 'I'll drive,' Clive announced. He hadn't driven since the onset of his illness.

'Fine,' Ruth said. They got into the car. 'Clive,' she

said, 'I do wish you'd reconsider the counselling service that Dr Singleton—'

'Oh, we don't want any of that "treat the whole family" social work nonsense,' Clive said dismissively. He leaned forward and switched on the radio, effectively ending the conversation.

Chapter 9

It was beginning to seem to Bill Stanhope that his wife could talk of nothing but the Gregorys. Even during what should have been a relaxed Saturday morning breakfast on their patio, she'd managed to find an excuse to bring up the subject he least wanted to discuss. 'Nice tribute to Martin from the candidate,' she said, gesturing at a story in the paper she was reading. 'I'm glad he could stay in the campaign.'

'Why shouldn't he?' Stanhope asked warily.

'Well, if it had got out . . . If it had been *this* constituency—'

'No one in this constituency would have *known* if it hadn't been for me.'

Annie looked up from her paper; she'd heard this before. 'Look: *I* think it's tragic. *You* think it's tragic. So does everyone. But people had to be given the chance to protect themselves.'

'There's no danger!'

'No one can say that, not even you. We all read the papers—'

'The papers get it wrong, mostly.'

'It's a simple case of better safe than sorry,' Annie said sanctimoniously. 'That's what Madge Pearson was saying yesterday about the charity shop. They all feel dreadful, but they've had to let Ruth go. They have their children to think of . . . themselves . . . their customers.'

'Have they started swapping bodily fluids at the charity shop?'

66

'What?'

'That's what spreads infection. Sperm and blood, mainly.'

Annie was taken aback, but only for a moment. 'You were worried enough to send our daughter to Switzerland, remember?'

'All right,' Bill admitted. 'I did the company's dirty work and I wanted her out of the way. But Clive has a certain right to confidence that I helped the company break.'

'What right?' Annie pondered the implications. 'It's not as if he could sue, is it?'

'I don't know.'

'Of course he couldn't! He'd ruin Martin's career, if he did. You can't start out in politics with that kind of dirt in the background.' Bill shot her a disdainful look. 'Listen,' she burst out angrily, 'Clive Gregory brought disease here! He brought it among *us*!' She turned back to her paper. 'If I were Ruth, do you know what I'd do? I'd take myself off to Majorca, somewhere cheap and warm, and sit it out.'

Clive waited beside his car on the country road, wondering whether Stanhope had received his letter and why, if he had, there'd been no acknowledgement. It was twenty minutes past the time he'd suggested they meet; he looked hopefully at each approaching car, but there was no sign of Stanhope. Perhaps he should give it up as a bad idea, try a different tack – approach the MD directly. He checked his watch again and was about to get back into his car when Stanhope's silver Mercedes came into view.

Looking distinctly apprehensive, Stanhope strode towards Clive with his hand outstretched. 'Oh, we shake, do we?' Clive said with mock surprise.

'Why not?' Bill asked.

'I'd've thought you'd know better. I'm the sort of person

67

who spits and gives policemen lethal bites.' He began to walk down the road.

Stanhope fell into step beside him. 'What can I do for you?' he asked.

'I don't know yet.' Clive spoke with studied casualness. 'What have you done so far?'

'I thought it best to stay out completely.'

'And have you?'

'What?'

'Stayed out completely? I mean, I know you stayed away from *me*, but that's not quite the same thing.'

'Your consultant said it only concerned him and your GP.'

'And do you know what they say now?'

'No,' Bill said apprehensively.

'They say I'm fit for work.'

Bill stopped in mid-stride, as though he'd spotted a land mine. 'Clive, for God's sake—'

'I couldn't travel, of course, no more high-powered stuff, but I can sit at a desk.'

'That's impossible.'

Clive had been prepared for this. 'Why?' he asked coolly.

Stanhope was shaking. 'You don't need me to tell you. You have a serious illness. And a short life expectancy—'

'What's *your* life expectancy?'

'Mine?'

'Yes. I don't *know* how long I've got. Six months is only an estimate. And I could be perfectly well for longer. I thought you'd read the literature. There are precedents in the company—'

'There's no precedent,' Stanhope broke in.

Clive had done his homework. 'Lance Bradley. He worked for more than a year in a corner of the office. His wife was eternally grateful; she said it saved his sanity, and hers.'

'Lance Bradley had cancer.'

Clive pounced and sprung the trap. 'That's what everyone in the company thinks *I've* got. Except you and me. So you can tell them it'll be perfectly all right.'

Stanhope stood motionless, cornered. 'Listen, Clive,' he said, fumbling for words, 'I'm afraid it's not that simple. You see, I had to . . . it was my obligation . . . it would have been irresponsible not to . . .'

'Not to what?'

'I had to tell the MD.'

'And who else?' Clive said with consternation.

'What?'

'*And who else?*'

'No one else!'

Clive snorted with disbelief. 'You want me to believe you told the Managing Director and no one else?'

'Yes. It was in the strictest confidence. I went to his house,' Stanhope said miserably.

'What about your wife?' Clive asked, pressing. 'Did you tell your wife?'

'Did you tell *your* wife company business?' Stanhope parried.

'I never had anything interesting to tell.'

By unspoken agreement, the men reversed direction and headed back towards their cars. '*My* wife got a letter from the golf club,' Clive said pointedly, 'saying she was released from committee work so she could devote all her time and energy to looking after me. Recognise the style?' He laughed hollowly.

'There are five members of the company board in the golf club,' Stanhope said. 'Geoff Parrish found out.'

Clive was aghast. 'How?'

'By putting two and two together, for God's sake! He only had to ask for the number of your ward in the hospital. People *talk*, Clive,' Stanhope said, not unsympathetically.

With an effort, Clive pulled himself together and tried to recoup. 'Even so . . .'

'What?'

'Tell them whatever they need to know. Tell them I'm safe, not infectious.' It was he who was cornered now. 'Imagine what it's like!' he implored. 'Every twinge, every sneeze. Is this it? Sealed off from Ruth, from the children – *I've got to have my job!*'

Bill spoke with genuine regret. 'What I tell them won't make any difference.'

'Yes it will . . .' Clive played his trump card: '. . . if I take you to court for breach of confidence.'

'I'd be exonerated!' Stanhope said with certainty.

'Oh. Taken advice, have you? Who said anything about winning the case? It'd be enough to embarrass the company. One of their executives with AIDS – Christ! Clients wouldn't like it.'

'It'd embarrass your family, too,' Stanhope said feebly.

'Leave my family to me.' Clive felt a surge of power. 'Tell the MD I'd consider a deal. A desk and an office for as long as I can work, and I'll keep quiet. In the meantime, there are some modifications to the demonstration model I can deal with at home.' He turned away from the stunned Stanhope and strode briskly towards his car.

Clive arrived home feeling euphoric, congratulating himself on how he'd played his hand. He was sure Stanhope had seen the light. They'd all see the light. They'd have to. He was, after all, an integral part of the team. They needed him as much as he needed them. Buoyantly, he joined Ruth and Nell in preparations for a family barbeque. Martin was expected; he hoped that, for a change, he wouldn't be late.

Visiting his parents' house for the first time in weeks, Martin noticed that the lawn, always meticulously trimmed and cared for, looked neglected and overgrown; a broken branch from a tree lay in the drive. He carried a bundle of washing from his car into the kitchen, where Nell was washing a lettuce in the sink. 'What happened to your hair?' was his greeting. The straight, silky strands she'd had since childhood had been transformed into a soft, trendy frizz.

'Nothing "happened" to it. I had it interfered with,' she said over her shoulder. 'Old pals don't recognise me, so they don't start talking till I'm out of earshot. Mum likes it.'

Through the window, Martin saw his father in the patio, wearing a cook's apron and tending the fire. 'We're doing Normal Family Life tonight,' Nell said flippantly.

Martin looked at Clive appraisingly; he thought he looked quite well, all things considered. 'How is he?' he asked.

'Why don't you come home more often and find out?'

'I do the best I can. Are things . . . bad?'

'Of course they're bad. They're terrible. He's decided to be "positive". He talks like a management training manual.'

'Doesn't anyone try to stop him?'

'He's got a lot of techniques for silencing the opposition. It's what he was paid for. Why don't you try?'

'Me?'

'Yes, Mart. You.' Avoiding her accusatory glare, he looked around the room and noticed that his mother's invariably spotless kitchen showed the same small signs of neglect he'd noticed in the drive. 'She used to go crazy if there was a fork out of place in here,' he mused.

'Yes. I had to make her see sense.'

'What do you mean, sense? What's the sense in letting things get out of hand?'

Nell smouldered with anger. How dare he come

waltzing in at his convenience and make judgements, criticize? 'It's do-it-yourself time now, dear. That goes for dirty washing, too.' As she spoke, the back door opened and Clive looked in.

'Martin!' he said jovially – too jovially, his son thought – 'you made it!'

Thrown by the unexpected conviviality, Martin managed an answering smile. 'Sorry I'm late, Dad. David had a Rotary Club tonight, and I was reshaping his speech.'

'Terrific!' Clive said with exaggerated enthusiasm. 'Terrific.' Without waiting for a reply, he returned to his cooking chores in the garden. Nell caught Martin's eye but said nothing, merely raising her eyebrows as Martin followed their father outdoors.

Clive's forced joviality continued throughout the meal, while the others strained to follow his lead. Martin began to wonder whether the evening would ever end. Finally, after his second cup of coffee, Clive inveigled Nell out onto the lawn for some croquet practice. By the glow of the barbeque coals, Martin poured two glasses of wine and handed one to his mother. 'I'm sorry,' he said quietly. She looked at him questioningly; her mind had been on potential last-minute sponsors for Morrie in the Joy Race. 'About what happened after the election. It looks as if it sparked something off.'

Ruth shrugged. 'We'd have had this stage anyway, wouldn't we?'

'Would we?'

'I think so. It has to run its course.'

'I want to tell *him* I'm sorry,' he said, his voice filled with remorse. 'About . . . everything.'

'He doesn't want to hear. Especially from you. Sorry means failure.' She peered at Clive through the gathering twilight. 'We're not "programmed" for failure.'

Martin lowered his head into his hands. He wants comfort. Ruth thought, and I can't give it to him; there's

72

nothing left in the account. 'Apart from all this,' she said, 'are you satisfied? Have you got what you wanted?'

His voice was muffled: 'More or less.'

'Good. So has Nell.'

Martin raised his head. 'A photography shop?' he asked dubiously. 'Don't you mind?'

'No.'

'Really?'

'Really. It's perfect.'

'And how about you? I rang you at the charity shop last week. They said you'd left.'

'Have you told your father?' she asked quickly. Martin shook his head. 'Good.' She reached across and took his hands, feeling empty and inadequate. 'Martin,' she said softly, 'I wish I could help you, but I can't. Let's just find our own ways through this, shall we? And come together when we need to?'

Martin nodded. He wasn't quite sure what she meant, but he felt, with grateful relief, that she'd released him from some indefinable hook.

Chapter 10

Becca was starting to wonder whether her membership in the golf club was worth the price – not the annual dues, but the unavoidable encounters with busybodies like Annie Stanhope, whose meddling apparently had no bounds. Whenever Becca appeared at the club these days, Annie seemed to seek her out, with unsolicited comments and questions. On this particular occasion, a sunny afternoon, Annie had followed her all the way from the eighteenth hole to the clubhouse while Becca, in conversation with her partner, tried to pretend she didn't see her. Outside the clubhouse, Annie caught up. 'Morning, Becca,' she said, aggressively.

Becca's partner, already late for a lunch date, deserted her. 'Hello, Annie,' Becca sighed.

'I just wanted to tell you,' Annie said self-importantly, 'we're having a bit of a crackdown this month.'

'We?' Becca asked, puzzled.

'The committee.'

'Oh. Yes.'

'And of course I don't want to come over all officious—'

'No?'

'—but the question of signing in games has come up.' She paused, choosing her words. 'Someone said you had a game with Ruth a week or so back—'

'That's right.'

'Well,' Annie said, gloating, 'it wasn't entered in the book.'

'We must have forgotten,' Becca said honestly.

'I understand it was very early in the morning,' Annie went on, 'so there probably won't be any repercussions this time. Though I'm surprised that Ruth could find the time. How is she?' she asked, her voice dripping with saccharine sympathy.

'Not bad, considering,' Becca said evasively.

'Good,' Annie said. 'I'm delighted. I hear the poor little daughter has dropped out of school . . . But Martin's still doing exceptionally well.'

'Yes,' Becca said, not trying to hide her impatience to be off.

Annie paid no notice. 'I hope Clive's activities don't affect that—'

'Activities?' Becca asked, wondering, *Is there no end to the woman's meddling?*

'Oh, threatening writs and things . . .' Annie said insinuatingly.

'I have an appointment,' Becca interjected.

Undeterred, Annie continued: 'He's something of a thorn in Bill's side at the moment. I wonder if Ruth's been put in the picture?'

Becca realised that a decision with which she'd been struggling for weeks had been made. 'You know, Annie,' she said, accepting what she suddenly knew had been inevitable, 'I really think I shall have to leave the club after all.'

Annie gasped, astonished. 'But you've only just been reinstated!'

'I'd've been *sacked* on your terms,' Becca said, 'I shall *leave* on my own. When I'm ready.' Feeling immeasurably lighter, she turned and walked away.

Ruth was surprised at how much she'd come to look forward to her afternoons at the ballroom; she was more comfortable there now, she realised ruefully, than at home, where the tension was constant, and building to a climax she dared not contemplate. Sometimes she envied Clive his ability to delude himself about returning to work, thinking that false hope must be better than no hope at all. Mostly, though, she tried to think about anything *but* Clive. Her efforts to line up sponsors for Morrie served that purpose wonderfully well. So did the dancing.

With the exception of Becca and Dennis, the ballroom 'regulars' knew as little about Ruth as she did about them – although she sensed that most of them were, like herself, emotional bankrupts. She found the anonymity oddly comforting, and relaxed in the knowledge that here, at least, nothing was expected of her except keeping the rhythm and avoiding her partner's feet. She sat sipping tea at a table with Dennis, watching Becca glide past in the arms of a Max Bygraves lookalike. Fraser sat at the next table, solemnly eating his usual ice cream. 'I don't know what I'm doing,' Ruth mused, thinking out loud. 'Clive set off in the car this morning and I didn't even ask where he was going.'

Dennis's attention was on Becca. 'Here's me got work in a carpet warehouse,' he said, 'and she keeps showing up on the half-days in her big car. Giving us treats. I suppose it's okay.' He nodded in Fraser's direction. 'I don't want him to be a crutch for a getting-over-it drunk.'

Edgar danced by, spotted Ruth and called out, 'You've halfed your dose!'

Ruth smiled. 'She'll know when to let go,' she told Dennis.

'At the warehouse,' he said deliberately, 'they think I'm knocking her off.'

'What?' Ruth asked innocently.

'She'd need to be awful fond of a bit of rough.'

His meaning sunk in; she realised he was trying to shock her. 'You're not that rough,' she said coolly.

He was amused. 'You've had worse, have you? Round the back of the clubhouse?'

'Stop it,' she said, as though to a misbehaving child. 'You won't outrage me.'

'No?' Dennis said sceptically.

'No.'

'Got to shine your own silver and suddenly you're a woman of the world, eh?' Before she could respond, he softened his tone. 'How's your old man? Still saying he never felt better?'

'Yes.'

The absurdity of their conversation, and of her mere presence in these surroundings, suddenly struck him and made him guffaw loudly. 'You get to take anything in the end, eh?' he observed.

Ruth hesitated only briefly. 'Even homosexuals?'

'What?'

'Now who's outraged?'

'Not *me*,' he said, his face going pink.

'You're embarrassed.'

'I'm not embarrassed,' he said angrily.

'You're embarrassed by the word. So was I. I don't think I've ever said it before.'

'Queers'll do,' Dennis sneered.

'That's what men of the world call them, like Clive.'

'You're trying to say he's one?'

'No,' Ruth answered calmly.

Dennis raised his voice. 'Queers are filth. It was a queer's blood they gave Fraser.'

It was Ruth's turn to be embarrassed; she looked around uneasily. 'It wasn't intentional,' she protested.

'Is that right?' Dennis struggled to contain his rage and despair. He stood up. 'Watch him, will you?' he murmured, indicating Fraser. He moved to the next table and abruptly asked an elderly woman to dance.

Ruth watched him, shaken, feeling strangely elated by what she knew was a tiny but definite victory.

*

Martin made his way up the rickety wooden steps to the photography studio, scarcely noticing the dilapidated surroundings that ordinarily would have appalled him. He was supposed to be working on Langley's speech, but his concentration was shattered by an ominous feeling of foreboding he couldn't discuss with anyone – except, perhaps, his sister. Martin had his father's analytical mind; it had paid off handsomely for him at Oxford. His faith in rational answers and practical solutions had, until recently, been unshakeable; now, he found himself unable to even define the questions. 'Let's find our own way through this,' his mother had said. He was trying, but emotions he'd always considered to be childish and contemptible blocked his progress; he felt utterly lost and alone. He tried to focus on his future – the job awaiting him in Hong Kong, now only two weeks away. If he could only hang on until then . . .

Nell was pinning up prints to dry and waiting for Nicky to get back with sandwiches when, to her surprise, Martin walked in. She stopped what she was doing and looked at him inquiringly, saying nothing. Ever since the night of the by-election, she'd felt bitterly disappointed in her brother. His single-minded devotion to his embryonic career reminded her too much of their father's attitude towards his work. And while Clive's illness had forced Nell to grow up in a hurry, Martin showed no sign of growing up at all.

He looked round the studio; she waited for him to comment on its seediness. Instead he said dejectedly, 'I've just been home.'

'What for? Did you need a shirt button replaced?'

'There was no one there.'

'If we'd known, we'd've got up a reception committee.'

'Oh, cut out the sarcasm. God . . . that place depresses me.'

'According to Dad, depression's a principle of bad management.'

'How is he?'

'The same. Acting as though everything will be back to normal any minute.'

'I keep thinking something terrible is going to happen.'

'It's already happened. How could it get any worse?'

Martin wandered about the studio, inspecting the photos that covered the walls. Nell reminded herself that he was probably doing the best he could – as they all were, given their limitations, in a situation where only change and pain were predictable. Her own job was all that was keeping *her* sane – but it was, after all, more than a job, her employer more than an employer. She'd never known anyone like Nicky – her parents had seen to that. His lifestyle, politics and family background made him as exotic to her as an Aborigine. But he was teaching her every aspect of the business, and they did get on well. However depressed she might be when she showed up for work in the morning, Nicky could always make her laugh. She pointed to a publicity photo on the wall. 'What do you think of my boss?'

Martin peered at the picture; a man of about his own age with a punk hairstyle, skintight trousers and an earring peered back, smiling with arrogant assurance. 'Looks a bit flash to me.'

'Well,' Nell said with mock derisiveness, 'he's probably Labour.'

'Does he know?'

'About Dad and AIDS? Yes. He doesn't give a shit, actually.' Martin winced at her language. 'I expect he's had it himself,' she said, enjoying his discomfort. 'He's had everything else, including me.'

'Stop it!' he pleaded.

'Oh, I'm going to. It's the smell of dope and polo mints, *together*—'

Her brother was as appalled as she'd intended him to be. 'Nell,' he gasped, 'you've got to hold on to something. To some kind of—'

'Standards? God, you'll be a wow at Brighton one day. You really will, Martin. Really,' she said her voice breaking. 'Really . . .'

Martin was horrified; his sister never cried. He put a tentative arm around her. 'It's been worst of all for you,' he said.

'It's the way they're so separate,' she sobbed. 'He's still in the spare room, of course. Or he shuts himself in the study to work. And she goes out.' He handed her his handkerchief and she blew her nose. 'Do you know what the worst thing is? It's thinking that there wasn't all that much between them before this happened.' She dried her eyes. 'She shouldn't have been so protected all those years, you know. She shouldn't have been able to *buy* protection.'

'What do you mean?'

'That's what they do — company wives. They buy themselves out of being disturbed.'

Martin wasn't sure what she meant. 'Where is she now?' he asked. 'Where does she go when she goes out?'

'I don't know. I think maybe she's getting interested in helping victims generally.'

'Not gays?' Martin asked, alarmed. Nell shrugged. 'It'd be logical, wouldn't it?' he said thoughtfully. 'If she could stomach it. Find out more about the disease . . .'

'I don't know,' Nell said. 'I don't think it matters.'

'As long as it's not going to be a Cause,' Martin said. His sister regarded him quizzically. 'I've got nothing against gays,' he explained. 'Oxford was stiff with them. But they're death at the moment. Politically. I mean, it's the one thing to have a laugh, but real contact, anything public, it's death.'

'Martin!' she said sharply. 'Get out of here! Go find yourself another Rotary Club, and join it!'

'I just thought that if she was,' Martin said nervously, 'I'd like to know.'

'Get out!' she said, thoroughly disgusted.

He looked at her helplessly: 'It's just that . . . I don't know what to do . . .'

'Get out,' she repeated tightly; 'I've got work to do.' *He's hopeless*, she thought, turning back to her prints. *Thank God for Nicky.*

Clive waited impatiently for the last Friday of the month; not until then could he put the next phase of his campaign to get back to work into action. The timing was crucial. He had to make his move before his team's planned demonstration of their system. He would approach his colleagues when they were relaxed, during their traditional monthly lunch at a restaurant near the office.

He watched from his car as the six men arrived, en masse; despite his apprehension, the sight of the men with whom he'd shared intense moments of triumph and disaster cheered him immensely. These men knew him better than Bill Stanhope ever could do. They'd been through so much together, good times and bad. They knew he'd done nothing that they hadn't done. They'd understand. They needed him. Carrying his briefcase, he followed them inside, then paused by the door, figuring he'd wait till they had their drinks before surprising them.

Oblivious to Clive's presence, the men considered the menu. Paddy wanted *moules*, George consommé: 'I had the squits something chronic in Delhi.'

'Ah,' Paddy recalled nostalgically, 'remember Bangkok?' He looked up and caught sight of the last person on earth he wanted to see. 'Jesus Christ!' His face fell in dismay.

'What?' Marcus asked, following his gaze. 'Oh, no! Jesus!'

'Christ, no!' Geofff Harris chimed in.

George Winters looked as though he'd seen a ghost. 'Clive Gregory – that's me off—' Hastily, he stood up.

'Sit down,' Geoff hissed.

'Sorry, Jan's pregnant. I don't take chances.' Winters turned and made for the back door of the restaurant as Clive approached briskly from the front. The other men watched, stunned, as Clive reached their table.

'Hello, you lot,' he said warmly. 'I'm glad to see the old tradition's still in force.'

Geoff was the first to regain his composure. 'What are you doing here, Clive?' he asked inhospitably.

'Surprised? How do I look?' Clive beamed. He had dressed with care, aiming to look the part of the successful businessman which, dammit, he was. He'd even managed to replace the hospital pallor with a bit of a tan.

'What are you doing here?' Geoff challenged him.

'It's the last Friday in the month!' Clive said jovially. 'We always have lunch, don't we? Those of us who aren't in foreign parts. Well, I've missed a couple, but I doubt if I'll need to miss any more.'

Geoff appointed himself spokesman for the group. 'Go home, will you?' he said quietly.

Clive was taken aback. 'What?'

'We're all sorry about what happened,' Paddy said, not unkindly, 'but we don't want you here.'

Clive's powers of persuasion were considerable; confidently, he drew upon them now. 'No, listen – I'm in remission! There's absolutely nothing to worry about!' He sat in the chair George had so hastily vacated, between Marcus Blackstone and Geoff. Reflexively, both men drew back.

Marcus gestured around the room. 'Look at this food!' he said, his voice rising with panic. 'He's a walking, sodding bag of germs!'

'Who told you that?' Clive asked, alarmed.

Geoff turned to Marcus, furious. 'Shut up and get out.' With obvious relief, Marcus complied.

Clive had expected some resistance, but nothing like

this. It wasn't going at all according to plan. 'Bill Stanhope could be in trouble,' he said, thinking out loud.

'The company'll look after him,' Geoff replied.

'No one's answered my letters.'

'We don't get your letters,' Geoff explained. 'They're stopped at the outer office.'

'The MD's, too?'

Paddy spoke bluntly, hoping to force Clive to recognise reality. 'A man in gloves incinerates them.'

Clive fought to remain calm. 'This rumour about infection—'

'Please leave,' Geoff broke in. 'Otherwise we'll have to—'

'—Whatever it is you think I've got,' Clive said urgently, 'I can't give it to you. Listen: I was going down with this for more than a year and you worked with me, *lived* with me. But you're all okay.'

'Apart from being right off girls,' Paddy muttered.

Geoff inspected his former colleague with sympathy. 'You've lost weight.'

'You were always telling me I needed to,' Clive joked feebly. No one laughed. He reached into his briefcase and brought out a file. 'I've been having a few thoughts on the Barford system. Last minute things, you might like to look them over. Just suggestions.' He put the file on the table. 'All that must be coming to the boil—'

'Well, the demonstration's next week,' Geoff stalled, frantically trying to find a way to end the discussion with a minumum of damage.

'Right on target,' Clive said heartily, misinterpreting his tone. 'I'm proud of you!' He smiled at the four men who remained at the table.

'Thanks,' Paddy said. Clive caught the irony and tried another tack.

'If I brought a case,' he said threateningly, 'there'd be publicity. Witnesses from within the company.' In silence, the men considered the implications of his words. 'Someone should remind the MD,' he went on. 'And you might put in a good word for me. We've had some great times together.' The men sat like stone, acknowledging nothing. Clive glanced at the headwaiter, who was hovering, and said, with forced heartiness, 'Now, let's order, shall we? And you can fill me in on what's been happening.'

Geoff could bear it no longer. 'Please go home,' he said.

Clive's bravado disintegrated. 'I've had enough of home,' he said pleadingly. 'I can't stand home. That's why we do this job isn't it?'

'Sorry,' Geoff said firmly. Looking everywhere but at Clive, he got to his feet and walked away from the table, the others following.

'Wait!' Clive cried out, pushing the file at Paddy. 'Look this over, will you?' Paddy flinched, as though fearing contamination; a sheaf of papers fell to the floor. Without a backward glance, the men left the room.

Clive bent down to retrieve his papers, aware that diners at other tables were staring at him with curiosity. Feeling utterly betrayed, exposed and profoundly alone, he sat at the table and buried his head in his hands.

Chapter 11

'He's about to get the biggest golden handshake ever,' Annie Stanhope reminded her husband; why couldn't he get it through his head that he had absolutely nothing about which to feel guilty?

'You're right, Bill said wryly, 'and the most rapidly arranged early retirement.' Every time they got in the car together these days, he thought, a row broke out – and the subject was always Clive Gregory.

'He's being *rewarded* for breaking the rules!' Annie said righteously. 'Ruth'll be absolutely *rolling* when he goes.'

'Goes?'

'Dies, I mean.'

Bill pulled the car into a parking place near a sign that read WEST BERKSHIRE ADVERTISER JOY RACE – FINISH. Routh Electronics had been asked, along with other companies in the community, to contribute to the charity event. Instead of money, they had donated the service of their company doctor.

Bill opened his door, but Annie wanted to make sure she'd made her point. 'All I'm saying is, I'm tired of hearing about how guilty you feel. You did what was necessary to protect your own job. What else could you have done?'

'Nothing,' he conceded. 'But he does have a point.'

Scanning the crowd, Annie spotted a familiar face. 'Is that David Langley over there?'

'Yes. He's giving the prizes. It was supposed to be someone from the Archers, but he had to cancel.'

'He'd be worth knowing,' Annie advised her husband. 'See if you can have a word at some point.' Looking exceedingly glum, Bill moved to get out of the car. 'And cheer up before tonight. I don't fancy gazing at that face across the Goldman's dinner table.' He sighed. 'Bill,' she said, reading his mind, 'he *won't* go to court!'

Stanhope was unconvinced. 'He might if his strength lasts.'

Annie shook her head. 'There's bound to be a way of shutting him up.'

'The hospital tent's over there,' Bill said. 'I'll see you back here, later.' She nodded. As he moved into the crowd of first aid helpers and other officials, David Langley walked past the car with Martin Gregory just behind him. Annie called 'Martin!' and got out of the car.

Martin paused, looking disconcerted. 'Hello.'

'How are you, Martin?'

'I'm fine.'

'You're doing extremely well,' she said unctuously, 'We always knew you would . . .'

'Thanks,' he said, searching for an escape route.

'. . . in spite of the tragedy,' she continued. 'Bill's here this afternoon, you know.'

'No,' he said, 'I didn't—'

'He's in charge of the hospital tent. His good deed. He's been very worried about your father – especially since this new development about taking action.'

Martin felt panic rising. 'Action?'

'Mmm,' Annie said knowingly. 'I'd've thought making the whole thing more . . . *public* couldn't be good for anyone. I've told Bill to stop worrying. I'm sure you'll all make him see sense.'

Confused by the speed of events, torn by conflicting loyalties, Martin turned abruptly away and plunged into the crowd, searching for Langley.

In her kitchen, Ruth filled a flask of coffee and wondered whether she'd overlooked any other last-minute preparations for the Joy Race. It was nearly two o'clock – later than she'd thought. Scott would be wondering what was keeping her.

As she grabbed her coat and hurried towards the front door, Clive rushed down the stairs, also in a hurry. He was dressed as though for work, in business suit and tie, and carried his briefcase. 'Where are you going?' she asked, surprised.

'I don't want to bother you.'

'You won't bother me,' she assured him. 'Do you want to know where *I'm* going?'

'I haven't time now, Ruth,' he said; he started past her, towards the door.

'No time to talk?'

'I can't afford the kind of talk you want,' he said agitatedly. 'I have to clear up this misunderstanding I had with the team the other day—'

Ruth saw a wild look in his eye; she spoke gently. 'They won't take you back, Clive.'

He shook his head, refusing to listen. 'Let me concentrate on what it is I'm trying to do!'

'Please,' she said, sensing danger, 'come with me. I've met some new people—'

'Sorry. It's the last push.' He searched his pockets for his car keys.

'Sometimes I wonder,' Ruth said, acknowledging defeat, 'what would've happened if you'd gone on to retire in the normal way. Would we ever have had anything to say to one another?'

'I'd hoped to drop dead on the job,' Clive said. 'Good fast coronary in the board room.'

Ruth was shocked. 'Do you mean that?'

'Yes,' he said, as though stating the obvious.

'Then . . . what's been wrong with us?'

Impatient, he shook his head and went out of the door. She followed; in their respective cars, they drove off in opposite directions.

Ruth pondered their conversation on the way to the Joy Race, but the scene that greeted her at the starting point pushed everything else out of her mind. Amidst great camaraderie, competitors were lining up – some in wheelchairs, some quite elderly, some jokey runners in outlandish outfits and other runners whose disabilities, if they had them, were not apparent. She spotted Scott and Morrie, both in their running gear; making her way towards them, she was pleasantly surprised to see that Becca, who had volunteered to come along as moral support, had brought Dennis and Fraser with her. Dennis looked dour, but Ruth hadn't time to wonder why.

Morrie's supporters held a hurried consultation. 'I'll be at the halfway point to pick you up,' Ruth told Scott. 'Dennis and the others will be further on if Morrie needs anything.'

Dennis glowered at Morrie, who grinned. 'Thanks, Dennis, but I won't.' Dennis nodded curtly and walked away, ostensibly to keep an eye on his son.

'Queer-basher . . . ?' Morrie muttered cheerfully.

Scott turned to Ruth. 'How much is on him now?'

'A hundred pounds a mile,' Ruth said triumphantly.

Scott whistled in admiration. 'Jesus! Who made it round figures?'

'The vicar. I played on his guilt about Clive.'

Scott put an arm around Morrie's shoulders and squeezed affectionately. 'That's you, then, isn't it? You're going for a thousand quid.'

Morrie gave his lover a searching look. 'I'm really doing it for you, aren't I?' Restless, he skipped away.

'He's a good lad.' Scott said, 'You can't see his bumps, can you?' he asked anxiously.

'No,' Ruth assured him.

'I clocked a few more on his back this morning, in the shower. He hasn't seen them yet.' Ruth saw his optimism flag, saw him reinflate it. 'Come on,' he called out to Morrie, 'let's have a bit of limber!'

Ruth joined Dennis, whose expression was even darker than before. 'Getting to be a great con, aren't you?' he said, furious.

'Dennis—'

'Running for haemophilia!' he said scornfully. 'Who else did you take?'

'Commercial sponsors, mostly,' she said levelly, 'from my respectable charity days.'

'Who don't know about your old man?'

'That's right.'

'Getting a thrill from going illegal?'

'Not particularly.'

'Well, if this is togetherness,' he said grimly, 'I'm not playing. Bloody perverts—'

Ruth tried to explain. 'I was lonely. So were you. So are they—'

Dennis nodded toward Fraser. 'Listen, he's been put out of school twice. He'll bloody soon get put out again if it gets around that his Dad's well in with a couple of queers, one of them with AIDS.'

'You might need *their* support one day,' Ruth argued.

'Not me,' he said with certainty. 'Not theirs.' Before Ruth could answer, they heard the crack of the starting gun.

Clive drove to the station and took the train, wanting to arrive at the office looking as fresh as possible. He'd gone over last week's scene in the restaurant obsessively, analysing every word, every inflection, and concluded that he had obviously misjudged the opposition; his mistake had been in messing about with underlings. It had never occurred to him before, but perhaps they were

89

jealous of his abilities. He revised his strategy: this time he'd go straight to the top, as he should have done in the first place. If the MD hadn't seen his letters, well, he'd make his point in person – dispel the rumours, show himself to be fit for work.

He paused at the entrance to Routh Electronics, weak with nervousness; making a huge effort, he threw his shoulders back and walked through the door, feeling a rush of adrenalin. Instantly, a uniformed commissionaire barred his way, saying, 'Can I see your pass, please, sir?'

Clive stared at him in astonishment. 'Don't be ridiculous, Tom. You know me—'

'I'm afraid I've no authority to let you in,' the official said, uncomfortable but firm.

'It's Clive Gregory! I'm with the Managing Director's group, for the demonstration—'

'The Managing Director hasn't arrived yet, sir.'

'No,' Clive said quickly, 'but I can wait for him inside—'

'I'm sorry,' the commissionaire said, still blocking his way. He nodded to a security man, who moved towards them.

'This is crazy!' Clive protested.

'Why don't you wait over there, sir?' The official indicated a seat in the corner. 'We'll get someone to talk to you.' Clive stood his ground. The commissionaire and the security guard exchanged worried glances as Clive saw, through the building's glass facade, that the Managing Director's chauffeur-driven limousine had pulled up. Several men got out and entered the building; Clive hastily approached the one in the lead and grabbed his arm. 'Charles! I knew I'd get you at the demonstration. I just wanted to say hello, show you I'm fit—'

The Managing Director stopped momentarily in his tracks, then shook Clive off and plunged ahead, shepherding his companions with him. Clive tried to fall into step with them; '—and then have a quick word,' he entreated, desperate now. 'I tried writing, of course, but I thought that if you saw me—' He gestured wildly with his briefcase. 'Just a quick word about possible developments, Charles. Then I could talk to the group around the system, if you like. I've had a few last-minute thoughts.'

'Where the hell is Security?' the MD asked the commissionaire, painfully conscious of his VIP visitors' curiosity.

'You don't need Security,' Clive broke in. 'It's perfectly all right! Surely Bill Stanhope told you—' He found himself surrounded by three security guards and the commissionaire, all of them blocking his way and all trying not to touch him. The Managing Director disappeared into the lift with his party.

The four men hustled Clive back against a wall. 'Where's your car, sir?' one of them asked.

Clive could barely speak: 'I came on the train.'

The commissionaire glanced back at the unguarded entrance. 'This place is probably filling up with Arab terrorists.'

'Well,' said one of the security men, indicating Clive, 'we can always set *him* on them, can't we?'

With chilling efficiency, another company limousine was brought to the front entrance. Utterly beaten, his last reserves of energy going, Clive followed the men out to the car. 'This is what happens when rumour gets out of hand,' he muttered. The men contemplated the glass panel that separated the driver from the back seat.

'Let's get him in through the back,' the commissionaire said.

'That's where he's been, isn't it?' a security guard sniggered, his meaning lost on Clive.

'It's quite unnecessary,' he said, clinging vainly to a last shred of dignity, 'but if that's how you want to do it . . .'

'Fine,' said the commissionaire. 'This way.' Gingerly, he took Clive's briefcase.

'No!' Clive said grabbing at his briefcase. 'This is quite controversial stuff. I'd better hold on to it.' The official hastily threw the briefcase into the back seat; the other men almost viciously bundled Clive in after it. One of the guards jumped into the front seat, next to the driver. As the car sped away, he slammed the glass panel shut, and held it tightly in place with his hand.

Ruth waited at the halfway point as the runners came into view. Morrie was going strong; Scott, running beside him, was clearly tired. Seeing Ruth, he dropped out, but shouted encouragement after Morrie. 'Keep going! Keep going! You're strong! You're fine! Nice pace!' He sank to his knees and rolled over on the grass verge. 'He's going to do it!' he said joyously. 'He's going to do it!'

Ruth smiled and poured him some coffee from her flask. Not for the first time, she was moved by his devotion to the younger man. Love was the only word for it. How dare Dennis, or anyone, condemn them for that.

Scott jumped to his feet. 'Come on,' he called, 'there's a short cut to the finish line!' Ruth followed him through the crowd. At the finish line, the winners of the main event – not Morrie's – had already been declared. David Langley was congratulating the exhausted competitors; with a flicker of surprise Ruth saw Martin at his side and, beyond them, Nell, busily photographing winners and losers. Scott checked his watch. 'He should've been here by now,' he said anxiously, 'if he'd kept his time.'

'He's bound to be slower than in practice, isn't he?' Ruth reasoned. Behind her, Dennis threaded his way through the crowd, followed by Fraser and Becca. He took Ruth's arm and led her aside. 'He wasn't looking so good at the turn.'

'We called to him but he wouldn't stop,' Becca said, concerned.

'Okay,' Dennis said abruptly, 'that's me, then.' He looked round for Fraser, ready to leave.

'Dennis has got the heterosexual sulks,' Becca said, for his benefit.

He turned back, furious. 'Listen: you can quit being Lady Bountiful. I don't want you or her coming round us again. I've stopped playing drop-outs.' Spotting Fraser, he started towards him; Becca shot Ruth a worried glance and followed him.

Ruth turned back towards the finish line as Morrie came into view, still running with great difficulty. With bystanders shouting encouragement, he lurched dangerously towards the finish, seeming on the verge of collapse. 'We must go to him!' Ruth cried.

Scott held her back. 'Leave him!'

'Stay back!' Morrie gasped. The crowd roared.

'Come on, you!' Scott shouted hoarsely. 'Pick your bloody feet up! What do you think we've been doing all this time? Come on . . . Come on! Move it, will you?'

Out of the corner of her eye, Ruth saw her daughter kneeling beyond the finish line, pointing her camera at Morrie as he flung himself, finally, across the line and into Scott's arms, where he lay motionless. 'Come on, boy!' Scott said, heedless of the first aid volunteers who gathered round. 'You did it! You did it! Come on, get a grip of yourself!'

Behind her, Ruth heard David Langley's booming voice. 'Well done! Very courageous! Everything all right? Oh, Mrs Gregory!' he said. She turned. 'Look, Martin – your mother's here!' Martin looked at his mother with consternation. 'This a young friend of yours?' he asked Ruth. 'He's not disabled, is he?'

Bill Stanhope bent over Morrie, pulling down his eyelids, feeling his pulse. He reached down to lift Morrie's running vest, but Scott restrained him.

'No!' Scott said, alarmed. 'Leave it!' But Stanhope had already seen the raised purple blotches on Morrie's neck. Looking up, he saw Ruth's face; it told him everything.

He called for a stretcher but before it arrived, Morrie began to groan and opened his eyes. 'I should bloody well think so!' Scott said, breaking the tension. 'Come on, Morrie! Morrie!'

Morrie coughed weakly. 'Did I get there?'

'Yeah!' Scott exclaimed, hugging him. 'You got there, boy!'

'He may need a checkup,' Stanhope cautioned Scott. The two men helped Morrie to his feet. 'We know where to go, if necessary,' Scott told the doctor.

Ruth was weeping with relief. 'Take him to the car,' she said.

'That's all right then,' Langley said. 'Not disabled? Has he been ill?'

Annie Stanhope stood near her husband, watching and listening intently. She saw Bill react to the telltale blotches on Morrie's skin, saw Ruth's face, and an intuitive flash. 'What are you doing?' she asked her husband agitatedly. 'He's—' Stanhope shook off her hand and, with Scott, began helping Morrie in the direction of Ruth's car.

Martin stood at the edge of the crowd, torn by conflicting emotions. He heard his mother's reply to Langley: 'Yes, he has been ill.' He heard Annie Stanhope tell Langley, in a voice shaking with fury, 'There's something very irresponsible going on here.' He saw his sister lower her camera and look at him in despair. The cloud of confusion that had surrounded him for weeks suddenly lifted, and he knew exactly what to do. Making a huge effort, he stepped forward and addressed Langley in a voice that carried well beyond the MP. 'I suspect he has AIDS . . . like my father.'

An hour later, Ruth was hosting an impromptu victory celebration for Morrie, Becca, Fraser, a chastened Dennis and her two children. Martin's announcement had gratified her more than she could say; it had given her the courage to ignore the crowd of onlookers and tell the stunned Langley how much her family and other AIDS victims would appreciate his support. Not surprisingly, he'd mumbled something about writing to him at the House of Commons and practically *run* from the scene. Nonetheless, she'd tried.

Nell was making sandwiches, Martin pouring drinks, the others playing croquet, when Ruth heard a car in the drive. She thought immediately that it must be Clive, and hurried to meet him, eager to introduce him to her new friends. The sight of the car confused her; it wasn't Clive's, but a black limousine. A crumpled figure got out of the back seat and walked uncertainly, almost stumbling, towards the house. Shocked, she recognised Clive and ran to him, as the car drove swiftly away. He looked disoriented, and desperately ill – years older than when he'd left the house a few hours earlier.

'That was a company car . . .' he said vaguely. 'Mine's at the station . . . I left it . . .' He seemed stricken, absolutely defenceless. Calmly, very much in control, Ruth took his arm and gently led him into the house.

Chapter 12

Martin's 'coming out', as Scott called it, seemed to free the whole family from any further need for pretence, with themselves and with each other. Priorities shifted dramatically, with keeping-up-appearances pushed clear off the list.

The tragedy that had almost destroyed the family now brought them together, a tight little circle in an increasingly hostile environment. On the street and in local shops, acquaintances avoided Ruth and strangers stared. There were anonymous notes, vicious and crude. After the third one, Martin assumed responsibility for finding a townhouse where his mother and sister could live, away from the harrassment and nearer to the hospital.

The debacle at Routh Electronics had brought on a relapse that sent Clive back to the NHS hospital, debilitated and defeated. To his surprise, he found a kind of peace in defeat; at least it relieved him of the strain of deluding himself. He'd thought life without work not worth living; now he discovered how pervasive the habit of living could be.

Seeing Martin off for Hong Kong had been an emotional but necessary ordeal. It was common sense, not nobility, that made him insist that his son seize his opportunity. The alternative – to take part in what could be a prolonged death watch – was unthinkable. Clive already carried the guilt of Martin's aborted political career; he wouldn't add to it by allowing any further sacrifices.

After a lifetime amongst movers and shakers, Clive found himself now in a world of watchers and waiters. His bleak institutional room was infinitely depressing; the dayroom, where patients stared catatonically at the television screen, was even worse. Clive, who had always considered introspection unproductive and self-indulgent, now had the energy for little else. Regret filled his thoughts and his dreams; he sometimes awoke in the night, weeping. But despite Singleton's repeated suggestion that he avail himself of the hospital's counselling service, he could not bring himself to reveal to a stranger what he'd trained himself not to reveal even to himself.

He discovered a few small pleasures: a radio play when he could concentrate, classical music when he could not. His most significant pleasure was an unexpected one: the frequent company of his daughter. Clive hoped that she sensed what he lacked the emotional vocabulary to tell her: how much he looked forward to her visits, and how profoundly grateful he was for her understanding and support. She was so like her mother, but tougher, and she'd made it clear that she bore him no grudge.

On this grey October afternoon, Nell sat beside him in the day room, watching the television set with great interest. An anonymous woman, shown only in silhouette, was calmly revealing to the world her family's firsthand experience with AIDS. The woman was Ruth.

Her appearance on the programme had been Singleton's idea. When she'd refused, Singleton hadn't tried to convince her. He waited, hoping she'd convince herself. Very quickly, her outraged sense of fairness overcame her self-consciousness. The inconceivable became the inevitable, and she agreed.

With a few other patients and members of staff, Clive and Nell listened attentively. Ruth spoke haltingly at first. 'I was quite unprepared for the hostility we encountered from my husband's employers, from colleagues, people we'd thought of as friends. It was particularly hard for our children – although they've shown great courage, adapted, made changes in their careers.' Clive took Nell's hand and squeezed it. 'Whatever my husband did to contract the disease, it was no different from what any businessman away from home might do, having been under strain, then drinking too much, in company, and being offered a certain kind of outlet.'

The interviewer asked, 'Do you feel any bitterness towards homosexuals?'

Ruth hesitated only for an instant. 'No. I think our problem is the same as theirs.'

'And the same as that of haemophiliacs who received contaminated blood?'

'In the sense that we all have to fight the same disease – and the same prejudices.' She paused. When she resumed, her voice was stronger, more confident. 'I wish it could be understood that AIDS is difficult to catch; most people are in no danger. And discriminating against sufferers only helps to spread panic.'

The face of the programme's presenter filled the screen. 'Our thanks to this wife of an AIDS victim and also to Trevor Singleton, whose introductory comments were recorded earlier today – the day when this serious issue is once again under discussion in the House of Commons.'

The atmosphere in the ward relaxed; Clive hugged his daughter. 'That was hard for her, wasn't it?' he said.

'Not as hard as all that.'

'She's come a long way. Left me behind.' He looked to his daughter for reassurance.

'You're doing fine, Dad.' She patted his arm. 'Where now? Back to bed?'

'Well,' Clive said wearily. 'I don't think it's a disco night, do you?'

She grinned; arm in arm, they started out of the day

room. As they reached the door, a voice behind Clive asked, 'Was that your wife?'

He looked over his shoulder at the speaker, a pale, wraith-like girl of about Nell's age who lounged in a reclining chair, smoking, an insolent expression on her face. 'Yes,' he answered, 'it was.'

'Stupid bitch!' the girl muttered.

Clive winced. A nurse, attending to another patient, looked up: 'That's enough, Charlotte,' she said sharply.

Nell tugged at her father's arm and they moved on into the hall and towards Clive's room. 'Who's the posh screwball?'

'She's an addict, I believe,' Clive said. 'Or was. Seems even the rich can't avoid dirty needles.'

'She looks about my age.'

'And unlikely to get much older.'

'That bad?'

'Not yet. But they say she won't eat.'

They reached Clive's room. Exhausted by the effort of walking, he sank onto his bed. 'Awful places, these.'

'It's only for a rest. Till we get the house straight.'

'Yes,' Clive said drily. He made an effort: 'How's work?'

'Not bad,' she said, pleased to be asked. 'I'm getting a name for doing artistic weddings.'

'Artistic?'

'No groups. All holding hands and running through wet grass, in soft focus.'

'I seem to have underestimated everyone,' Clive said apologetically.

Nell leaned over and kissed his cheek. 'Mum said she'd try to come in before lights out.'

Clive shook his head. 'Tell her no – she'll be tired after today. And say well done, will you?'

Ruth wasn't tired, she was exhilarated. During the drive to the television studio with Singleton she'd wondered whether, despite her willingness, she could go through with it. Even though her face would be hidden, anyone who knew her would easily recognise her voice. She'd had to do it, though – and now she'd survived it. And Singleton, driving her home again, said, 'You were first rate.'

She looked out of the window and realised he was pulling into a car park near where she lived. 'The zoo?' she asked.

'It's a treat. Before I drive you home.'

Pleasantly surprised, she followed him through the entrance. 'I haven't been here since the children were little,' she said as a crocodile of small children wound past them, greatly excited.

Singleton peered upward as the sun made its first appearance of the day. 'Tea first?' he asked. At a table in the open air cafe, he congratulated her again. 'It was brave.'

She shrugged. 'I had nothing to lose.'

'No? The papers'll be on to it; there'll be the usual ignorant comment. Your erstwhile friends will have recognised you.'

'They've done their worst already.'

'Have they?'

'Well, I'm not such an easy target now I've changed sides,' she said sipping her tea. 'That's probably *why* I changed sides.'

Singleton leaned forward. 'I'd hoped you were more committed. So I could ask you another favour.'

She eyed him warily. 'What favour?'

'There's a need for a coordinated information service. Money's available. Out of small-scale government panic. I want to start with an exhibition – *AIDS in Perspective*, something like that.' Ruth guessed what was coming and shook her head. 'You'd be a very "respectable" spokesperson . . . though you wouldn't be anonymous for long.'

Ruth remembered the stares, the theatening phone calls, the obscene notes. 'No,' she said. 'It would be like putting a bell round my neck . . .'

Singleton played it cool. 'Think about it.'

'No,' she repeated, less firmly this time. 'I can't . . .'

'Finished your tea?' the consultant asked. 'Let's go for a walk.' He kept her engaged in conversation while he led the way past the aviary, past the reptile house, past the amphibians. 'I could use your energy,' he said.

'I don't know . . . I'm not sure what I'd be defending . . .'

'Talk to your gay friends.'

Your gay friends. That's what they were, of course – but she thought of them now as Scott and Morrie. 'I have. I'm sorry for them. But there's a kind of general . . .' she faltered.

'Distaste?' Singleton stopped – by design? she wondered later – beside the chimpanzees' compound, where chimps of all sizes, from babies to brutes, lazed in the sun. He nodded towards a large male chimp who glared back at him. 'Sex education. When he's in the mood, he'll take the nearest female backside that's offered to him. If he's really in the mood and the nearest backside happens to be a male one, he'll take that – as long as the other chap'll cooperate. Especially if they're all in the wild and the females happen to be a few yards further away. Although even in here it's not uncommon . . . If there were only males in this compound, they'd avail themselves of one another as often as they needed.'

Ruth blushed deeply, but stood her ground. Better a late sex education than none at all, she told herself. 'Where's this leading?'

'It's leading to a consideration of "unnatural acts". Aren't they really what bothered you when you found out about Clive?'

The knot in her stomach, absent for weeks, made itself felt again. 'I'm not sure I can take this . . .'

'Of course you can take it,' he said. 'You can take anything now, surely? "Unnatural acts" bother a great many people.' He gestured towards the chimp, who loped over to another chimp – his mate? With intense concentration, they began to groom each other. Ruth watched them, her embarrassment escalating. 'The urge to reproduce,' Singleton went on, 'has been served up in an ecstatic experience to make sure that we get on with it. As long as he hits the right spot more often than not, the future of the chimpanzees is okay. That's all nature requires. There are no "unnatural acts" for him, only outlets for his sexual drive.'

'He's an ape!' Ruth protested.

'And enough like us in his DNA – his life-stuff – to tell us something about ourselves. Now: we've socialised and commercialised our instincts to such an extent that we tend to feel comfortable in mutually excluding groups like "heterosexual" and "homosexual" – but real sexuality takes account of both, in each of us, at some level. Not in the same proportions. But circumstances will decide which part predominates.'

Ruth pondered the information; when she spoke, her question was tangential. 'Clive said it was with a woman, and just once . . . Is that likely?'

It was Singleton's turn to be fazed, but he didn't show it. 'Statistically, no. Though possible. There are documented cases.' She looked at him dubiously. 'Is it important?'

'Important? I lived with him for twenty-five years!' *Was it a girl?* Clive hadn't answered, and she'd not had the courage to ask him again. What kind of secret life had he had all those years?

Singleton was, as usual, direct: 'He wouldn't be the first man to try whatever happened to be on offer after a few drinks. You said it yourself, on television . . .'

'Yes, but . . . if certain kinds of behaviour lead to disease, they must be wrong.'

'Certain kinds of sexual behaviour may lead to disease, in which case they should be discouraged.'

Ruth looked perplexed. 'Doesn't it come to the same thing?'

The consultant shook his head. 'For me it's a health question, not a moral one.'

As though on cue, to illustrate the lecture, a chimp in the centre of the compound casually mounted his nearest neighbour. Ruth forced herself not to look away. Watching her, Singleton asked, 'What do you say?'

She knew he was returning to his original question; she didn't say yes, but she couldn't say no. Instead, she answered obliquely. 'I wish I knew more about ecstatic experience.'

'It isn't a requirement.' He began to lead her back the way they'd come. 'Oh,' he said, 'an afterthought. We think the virus may have begun among the green monkeys of West Africa . . .'

Bill Stanhope switched off the television set and poured himself a fortifying drink. Annie was already on the phone, galvanised into action by what she'd just heard on the news magazine programme. '. . . Of course it's irresponsible. Everyone round here will know who it was, so all that talk about "hostility from colleagues and friends" can only mean us . . . They're always one-sided, these programmes. They never give the other point of view. I suppose people are meant to put themselves at risk . . . Yes, well, I don't believe there's *no* danger . . . Precisely, that's what infuriates me. You'd think Clive'd done nothing at all to deserve it!'

Stanhope downed his drink, picked up a copy of the *British Medical Journal* and flicked through it to find the 'Appointments' page. Annie prattled on, oblivious to his darkening mood. 'He's dropped the idea of a case, thank God. It was never really on. And Martin saw what was what ... Mmmm, Hong Kong, I believe. Merchant banking. Till it blows over ... Yes, exactly, *lucky* ... He never had a *close* connection with Sharon, of course, she wasn't terribly interested ... Oh, I agree, awful. Though there was *something* – not exactly arrogance, but, you know – I mean, what did she *expect*? ... All right, see you on the twenty-second. Here's to the Revolution! Bye!' Laughing, she turned away from the phone as Bill poured himself another drink.

'Revolution?' he asked.

'I told you,' Annie said; you never *listen* to me any more! It's Louise's party, the twenty-second. Fancy dress on the theme of Revolution.'

Bill raised his glass. 'I'll drink to that.'

'The general impression is that Ruth's put the top hat on it,' Annie said with some satisfaction.

'Social death? Surely that doesn't matter. She hangs around with poufs now, doesn't she?'

The irony in his voice made her look significantly at his drink. 'Well, at least we've nothing more to fear from that quarter—'

'No,' he said mockingly. 'Thanks, Annie.'

'I suppose she's keeping the house because she intends to come back eventually,' Annie said, thinking out loud. 'The other place is rented. It must be costing them a fortune.'

'Still, they can afford it.' Restless, Stanhope got up and began pacing up and down the room.

'I think if she does come back, she'll find people have long memories. Though she'll never be able to sell it, will she? The house? Who'd want it?'

'I don't know. Someone from outside who hadn't heard, perhaps. A Pakistani surgeon, someone like that. Someone who'd cause the golf club committee even more heart-searching.'

'The rented house is nearer for visiting the hospital, I suppose,' Annie mused.

'So it's not just the way they were "hounded" out of the last one?'

He sounded positively surly, Annie thought; she was annoyed, and genuinely perplexed. 'I don't understand you, Bill. You're a success!'

'I helped to get a man who lives for his job retired,' he said, exasperated, 'when there was no reason why he shouldn't have carried on.'

'He's stopped agitating,' Annie ventured.

Bill blurted out the immediate cause of his guilt: 'He's back in hospital.'

'Well,' Annie said, surprised but undaunted, 'it's the best place for him, isn't it?'

'An NHS venereal ward? Of course. Just like the Hilton, but with no ice in the drinks. He caved in after that brush with the MD.'

'Why NHS? They must have decent insurance—'

'The private places don't want to know if you've got what he's got. Mind you,' he said sarcastically, 'he should've thought of that before he took his knickers off, shouldn't he?'

Annie's temper flared; as she started to speak, the phone rang. She went to answer it, leaving her husband to his drink and his medical journal. 'Hello? . . . Yes, incredible, wasn't it . . . *Honestly*, that's just what I've said to Louise . . . Everyone round here knew who it was and it does sort of implicate the rest of us . . . You know what I mean . . . Mmmm. He's back in hospital, actually. NHS, the other places won't touch him, it's so sad . . .'

Chapter 13

Clive stood by the window in the hospital corridor, watching Ruth make her way to the car park. She had come specifically to ask Clive whether he had any objections to her taking on the organisation of the AIDS exhibit; the more she had thought about Singleton's proposal, the more it appealed to her. All Clive could manage to say was, 'I'm grateful.' He had never been more proud of her.

From down the hall came sounds of uproar – the crash of crockery, an angry yell. Charlotte again, he thought. Singleton emerged from the day room, looking uncharacteristically upset. He paused when he reached Clive. 'Thought I'd try a little persuasion,' he said ruefully.

'Did it work?'

'How could it? She knows all the answers. Why should she eat and give the disease more flesh to work on? Ah, I missed your wife!'

'She's writing to you. We've been talking. We decided she should go ahead.'

Singleton smiled broadly. 'Thanks.'

'She has to do it,' Clive said. 'She says she'll do it until I can leave here.'

'Fair enough.'

'*If* I leave here. I'm worse, I think – don't you?' He spoke dispassionately, and got the straightforward answer he expected.

'Yes, but not critically.'

'I'd sooner Ruth thought I was improving.' Singleton nodded. '. . . at least for the moment.'

'There's a sense in which you're much better than you were, of course,' the consultant pointed out. 'You're accepting now.'

'If you mean that the fight's gone out of me—'

'It wasn't a fight, it was an obstruction. It took all your reserves.'

'You were very patient with me.'

'More so than with some of my patients, I'm afraid.' Singleton nodded in the direction of the day room, where Charlotte's caterwauling could be heard, her words indistinguishable. 'Goodnight,' the consultant said; he went on towards the lift.

Clive walked slowly towards the day room, stopping every few paces to catch his breath. He nearly collided with a nurse who was leaving the day room carrying a tray of food, angrily calling back over her shoulder, 'Please yourself, then Milady!'

Charlotte was silent when Clive walked in, languid in her usual reclining chair, smoking the ever-present cigarette. She watched as he picked up a newspaper and settled down to read. 'In ten minutes you'll put that down and walk back again,' she said scornfully. 'Why don't you read the paper in your room?'

Clive glanced up; the girl looked mored cadaverous every day, he thought, her huge sunken brown eyes seeming to fill her entire face. Her blonde hair hung below her shoulders, lank and unkempt. She wore an elegant blue silk Chinese dressing gown, embroidered with black and gold dragons. 'Last time I was in here I never left my room,' he said.

'So?'

'This time I promised my wife I'd, I don't know . . . take more part in the life of the ward.'

'What life?' the girl sneered.

Clive took the bait: '*You're* alive.'

'Where's your proof? Anyway, your wife is a stupid bitch.'

'So you said.' Clive couldn't be angry; she was too young to take seriously.

'What've *you* got in the way of family?' he asked, mildly curious. Her short life had obviously been a privileged one.

'Two bastards and a she-rat.'

'Seems appropriate.' What a little brat she is, he thought, going back to his paper. She laughed, genuinely amused.

'I'll take you for a real walk one day,' she told him.

'Where?'

'In this place.'

'You haven't the strength.'

'I've strength enough to walk.'

'But not to carry me.'

She looked at him meditatively. 'You know what I was just thinking?'

'What?'

'I had a nanny once who used to say, "There's always someone worse off than you are".' She giggled. 'Well, that's me, now – "someone". I should write and tell her.'

Clive affected boredom, as though teasing a spoiled child. 'What makes you think I'd want to walk with you?'

'Because you're quite snobbish in your Gautier dressing gown,' she said with a devilish gleam in her eye, 'and I'm reasonably well-educated and would amuse you.'

He laughed. 'I'd sooner talk to the porter about Luton's chances in the Cup.'

'That's a lie, Clive.' Anticipating his question she said, 'I know your name because I read your notes.'

She had his full attention now. Intrigued, he put down his newspaper and got to his feet. 'You can walk me back to my room, for a start. In my room there's a banana. You can eat it.'

'I don't eat,' she informed him.

'Then I don't speak to you.' As purposefully as he

could, he walked out of the day room. Behind him, Charlotte slowly unwound herself from her chair.

Ruth noticed that the band was playing 'Alice Blue Gown' – the song they'd been playing when Becca had taken her to the ballroom for the first time. Not that long ago, but it seemed years – in some ways, a lifetime. She was dancing with Dennis and using all her powers of persuasion to enlist his help with the AIDS exhibit. He wasn't having any. Disappointed, she said 'I thought you'd started to feel differently.'

'Okay,' he admitted, 'I was quite impressed with those gay guys. The older one, anyway. It's not that.'

'What, then?'

'The boy's getting a lot out of this new school. And they've not sussed, not even about the haemophilia.'

'Isn't it on his records?'

'I tidied up his records.'

Ruth was incensed. 'But you shouldn't have *had* to!'

'Right. But I'm taking no chances this time. I said he'd got brittle bones, so watch out for him falling, and call me if he does.'

'I need your help, Dennis,' she said. 'You of all people know how important it is to educate people—'

'No!' Dennis said forcefully. 'I'm not having anyone connecting us with AIDS. Also, I get one half-day a week and I like coming here.'

'Anyway,' Ruth said, adopting Singleton's tactic, 'think about it.'

They ended the dance and started back towards their table to join Edgar and Becca. 'I'm in the doghouse in that direction, too,' Dennis whispered, indicating Becca. 'She's mad because I'm letting the landlady do some babysitting. I thought she was getting too dependent.'

Ruth nodded. 'She said *she'll* give me all the help she can.'

Dennis refused to feel guilty. 'Great, take her mind off it. Funny how people with no jobs need their minds taken off things.'

At the table, Edgar rose to greet them. 'This is ours, I think,' he told Ruth as another waltz began. He led her back onto the dance floor and said, as they started to dance, 'Who's doing without her Valium, then?'

'Oh Edgar,' she laughed.

'I can always tell,' he said knowingly. 'Your steps have much greater definition. If you came two afternoons a week, you'd soon be more than passable.'

'I have to stop coming altogether, I'm afraid,' she said with real regret.

Edgar smiled. 'The times I've heard that! But most people come back . . .' With an extravagant dip and a flourish, they continued the dance.

Ruth found that organising the exhibit concentrated her mind and provided a channel for some of the anger she'd been unable to express any other way. Valium was a soothing pacifier; this was an energising challenge. Still hoping that Dennis would come around, she proceeded with a dedication and efficiency that far exceeded Singleton's expectations. The centrepiece, intended to illustrate that AIDS was above all a human, rather than political or moral issue, would be a stunning collection of Nell's photographs of Clive and Morrie, enlarged to life size, with appropriate captions. With Becca, Ruth approached potential sponsors and contacted health agencies for printed information to be given away. Scott, with his usual enthusiasm, offered whatever help he could give, on the condition that Morrie approved. He invited Ruth round to their flat for dinner, to discuss it.

She arrived a bit early, slightly nervous, though she couldn't think why. Scott was simply Scott to her now, a trusted friend and companion on a journey through treacherous territory, to a destination they both had every reason to dread. As he set the table in his tiny, tidy kitchen, she sipped her wine and curiously contemplated what was, after all, a perfectly ordinary domestic scene. What had she expected, she wondered – exotic decadence? Morrie was in the living room, absorbed in playing a video game on the screen of a computer terminal. Scott topped up her drink and started making a salad, chattering nonstop. 'My boss is gay, too, else I don't know what we'd've done. He fixed up the terminal for me and said I could work from home. Morrie does a bit too much of that, though; we kid ourselves we're going to design our own video game and make piles of money.'

'This project will involve some hefty correspondence,' Ruth said. 'Begging letters, mostly. We could use a computer.'

'You're welcome.'

'I thought,' Ruth said shyly, 'you two could take on the gay angle.'

Scott looked amused. 'Drawing the line, are you, Ruthie?'

She had an answer ready: 'You're better qualified.'

'I don't know about that,' Scott said doubtfully. 'There's a lot of paranoia around. Most of the local gays won't go near him. Still, at least that means he's faithful; hasn't got much choice. Though what's "faithful"? A goodnight kiss and me sleeping on the sofa. We tried counselling, but he wouldn't stick it.'

Ruth began to relax. 'Where did you meet him?'

'Morrie? Oh, one of them places. He put himself around a bit then. I was always at him to stay with me, but he wouldn't – till he collapsed.'

'Are you still training?'

Scott's face clouded over. 'He's had to take it easy since the race. Do you think he looks worse?' He didn't wait

111

for a reply. 'Took a bit of building up again, after the race. I think he's okay, physically. It's just his moods, you know.'

Morrie switched off the computer and joined them. He seemed tense. 'We're not back on the macrobiotic, are we?' he asked Scott contentiously.

'No, I told you—'

'Macrobiotics was his latest,' Morrie told Ruth, an uncomfortable edge to his voice. 'See him smacking his lips over the birdseed . . .'

'It was brown rice and millet,' Scott protested.

'Birdseed,' Morrie said with disgust. 'Yum, yum – full of vitamins . . .'

'And *him* nipping out for chocolate eclairs,' Scott interjected.

'Till I was caught. It was very nearly smack-botty time.'

Scott took a serious tone: 'Are we going in on Ruth's project?'

Morrie sulked. 'I don't know.'

Ruth turned to Scott. 'You, then, if Morrie doesn't want to.'

'It'd better be both of us or neither,' Scott said uneasily.

'Why?' Scott didn't answer. Ruth addressed Morrie directly for the first time: 'Nell's pleased with the photographs of the race.'

'Yeah?' he said guardedly.

'I said I'd ask you if we could use them in the exhibition.'

'What, me showing all me bumps? That'll pull the crowds—'

'For Christ's sake!' Scott burst in. 'You couldn't see your sodding bumps! I took care of that—'

'Just to show what can be done,' Ruth explained.

'You were beautiful that day,' Scott said.

Morrie turned away, determined to be difficult: 'Ah, don't piss me off!'

Ruth was also determined. 'We'll need captions,' she said.

'Captions?'

'Could you keep a diary?'

'*Write?* I can't write a letter!'

'On a tape recorder, if you like. Just your thoughts.'

'I don't have any thoughts,' he said obstinately.

'You do,' Scott protested. 'He does. So do I. We talk about it, don't we?' Morrie shrugged. 'We'll do it,' Scott said decisively.

'It'll be just another poxy routine,' Morrie said, pouting.

'The last one kept you going, didn't it?'

'Nothing's going to keep me off the slab in the end,' Morrie shot back, awash in self-pity. He turned to Ruth: 'Love gets a bit cloying, doesn't it?'

Ruth saw Scott flinch, wounded by the rebuff. Hastily, to end an awkward silence, she said, 'There's an adequate grant, and Clive says he'll do the accounting. I think that covers everything . . .'

Morrie withdrew into his sulk and wandered back to the video game. Ruth looked away from the desolation in Scott's eyes. 'It'll be all right,' he said, straining to believe it.

Chapter 14

Becca braced herself as she walked with Ruth through the graveyard to the steps of the picturesque old church where the vicar waited, hand outstretched. In search of community support, they'd so far succeeded in only three out of twenty-three tries, enlisting the support of a couple of Quakers and a Dominican monk. Becca badly needed a success; unlike Ruth, who seemed to have come to terms with her demons, Becca fought a daily, sometimes hourly, battle against despair. Hope was such a fragile commodity, in such short supply these days; she tried to choose her battles carefully, minimising the odds of defeat. This battle, however, was of Ruth's choosing. They had to try, she'd said, whatever the odds. The vicar had come to the house when he'd learned of Clive's illness; embarrassed, he'd offered to give them communion in their own "special" cup. Perhaps they could profit somehow from his guilt. 'God knows we need all the help we can get,' Ruth had said.

'Let's hope God's on speaking terms with the vicar.'

He greeted them saying, 'The Christian group is waiting,' and led them into the vestry. Five middle-aged men, seated round a table, looked up with barely suppressed hostility as they entered. 'Where are the women?' Becca asked.

'The mixed group didn't want to meet you,' the vicar said. He gestured towards some chairs. 'Please sit down. Now, if you'd care to state your request . . .'

'But it was all in our letter—' Ruth said.

'Yes, and we've discussed it at some length. But since you're here, perhaps you'd like to make a personal appeal . . .'

Brisk and businesslike, Ruth took a stack of pamphlets from her handbag and passed them around the table. The men accepted them with reluctance. This lot's just like the golf club women's committee, Becca thought – the same closed minds and hearts, only the gender was different. A truly 'Christian' group.

'. . . What we're anxious to set up,' Ruth was saying, 'is a network of sympathisers, if possible. Not just for counselling, but to bring together all groups who are most at risk.'

'And they are, again?' the vicar said.

Becca plunged in: 'Gays, drug addicts, haemophiliacs . . .'

The vicar cleared his throat. 'Well, I'm sure there's considerable sympathy . . .' he looked round the group for signs of assent; none was visible.

'I'd hoped there would be,' Ruth said encouragingly. 'We need names . . . supporters . . .'

The pudding-faced man on the vicar's left spoke up: 'I'm sympathetic, up to a point. But I must share my anger with the group as well.' There was a ripple of affirmative response.

'We're angry too,' Becca said quickly. 'There's so much ignorance, you wouldn't believe—'

'I'm afraid my anger wells up from a rather different source,' Pudding Face said.

The vicar strove for appeasement: 'Isn't it, ultimately, anger at the, er, folly of men?'

'Isn't ignorance folly?' Ruth said pointedly.

'Yes, indeed,' the vicar agreed. 'But then perhaps the original ignorance is harder to forgive.'

The man on the vicar's right had a grey beard and a distressing resemblance to Becca's ex-husband. 'The ignorance that leads people to *sin* – sorry for the word,' he apologised sardonically – 'in the first place.'

'People like Clive?' Ruth asked.

'We pray for Clive regularly,' the vicar assured her.

'Yes, I know, and we were grateful for your visit—'

A third man, a pasty-faced banker type, interrupted. 'The fact is, you want us to back the vicar to be on your platform, don't you?'

The vicar was wringing his hands. 'You see, I only have so much energy; it's a matter of where I place it . . .'

'Or where you're seen to place it?' Becca asked.

'The parishioners have a claim on the vicar's time,' the banker-type said smugly. Becca bit her tongue.

'We're parishioners – my family,' Ruth said. 'We supported the church.'

'And you'll have my support and prayers always,' the vicar replied.

'But not your name? Where it would do most good?'

'Oh, I think you're overestimating my influence. We've talked about this before, you know. That's why I wanted the group to meet you.'

Pudding Face spoke up: 'We've given the whole matter a thorough airing. And I'd sooner get back to talking about world poverty, quite frankly. The poor don't ask to be poor . . .'

A fourth man, hawk-nosed and haughty, joined in. 'We also felt that ancient wisdom may have been better informed than we know . . .'

Becca could no longer restrain herself. 'About what?'

'Sorry?' the man said, caught off guard.

'Oh,' Becca said, feigning enlightenment, 'about fornication, you mean? Sodomy? Buggery, that kind of thing?'

Silent, but furious, the members of the Christian group glared at Becca. The vicar looked terrified. 'It may be,' he said tentatively, 'that those prohibitions were founded on sound principles for good health—'

'—and disease is a punishment for sin,' Becca said; bored now, she was ready to cut her losses.

'Maybe it is,' Greybeard said defensively. 'Who are we to say it isn't?'

'Who's punishing haemophiliac children?' Becca asked.

Ruth spoke softly, directly to the vicar. 'You wouldn't have to change your views, Michael. You could argue them, compassionately, and still be part of the team. You're well-known here. People listen to you.' Her heart sank as he looked to the others for support that was not forthcoming.

'No, they wouldn't buy it, would they?' Becca said. 'They'd be taking their baptisms elsewhere and their wives'd be giving up the flower arrangements . . .'

'I'm sorry,' the vicar told Ruth. 'You're often in our thoughts.' He floundered for firmer ground. 'We're making a tremendous effort for world poverty at the moment, you see – it takes all my concentration, really.'

Becca got to her feet. 'Let's get out of here,' she said. To her amazement, Hawknose asked, 'Would you perhaps care to share your pain and disappointment with us?' She shot him a look of pure venom.

'Thank you for listening, anyway,' Ruth said, rising.

The vicar spoke mechanically: 'You're often in our thoughts. Shall we all sit quietly in church together for a few minutes?'

'No,' Ruth said, showing not a trace of the turmoil she felt. 'We have other people to see.'

'I'll see you out, then.' The vicar ushered them out of the vestry and stopped on the church steps. 'You do see my predicament?' he asked Ruth anxiously.

'Yes, I see,' she said, her mind already on their next appointment.

'And the group was rather smaller than usual . . .'

She smiled. 'I'm used to being avoided.'

'Ah, my bell ringers.' The vicar indicated a group of five or six people who were approaching the gate. 'I'd

117

forgotten. It wouldn't have been so easy to sit quietly in church, after all.'

Seeing Ruth, the women hesitated; one or two nodded to her, looking anything but friendly. 'Hello, Jennifer, how are you?' Ruth asked, all cordiality. The women nodded brusquely and pushed quickly past her. Ruth addressed the man behind her: 'And you, Ralph? All well with Sally and the children?' He looked away and hurried into the church. Ruth and Becca exchanged a glance that spoke volumes and started towards the car.

'Wait,' the vicar called, catching up. 'Er . . . look,' he said, wringing his hands again, '. . . I'll speak to the Bishop about this.' Gratefully, Ruth touched his arm. He followed the bell ringers into the church.

'Speaking of punishment,' Becca murmured, gesturing towards the gate, 'look who's here.' Annie Stanhope, carrying a huge harvest festival loaf baked in the shape of a corn stock, was coming their way. They watched as she recognised them and braced herself.

'Hello, Ruth,' she said, tight-lipped. 'Hello, Becca.'

'Whose mouth did you take that out of?' Becca asked, indicating the loaf.

Annie strained to be civil. 'It's for the Harvest Festival. Have you seen the vicar?'

'Yes,' Ruth said, 'we saw him.'

'I know he's been worried about you,' Annie said, dripping with solicitude.

Ruth decided to take her on. 'Really! You have the vicar's confidence now, do you? You've made such an impact since you came to live here, Annie.'

'I wouldn't call it an impact,' Annie said cautiously.

'Wouldn't you? You seem to be everywhere. What was it you said that day . . . ?'

'What day?'

'"You have to put something in if you want to get something out." What have you put in, Annie?'

Annie's eyes narrowed. 'Plenty.'

'—apart from ill-informed talk?'

'I'm not the only one who's been concerned,' Annie said belligerently.

'I think you were the first, though. To be really "concerned".'

'I don't know what you mean.'

'I mean,' Ruth said, glacial and in complete control, 'all this "concern" has made things much, much worse than they need have been. I'd like you to know that. I'd like you to feel it.'

Annie looked like a fox run to earth. 'This is starting to sound like slander,' she stammered.

'Is that the voice of authority?' Becca asked. Furious, encumbered with the absurd loaf, Annie went on towards the church. Ruth and Becca started again for the car. Cleansed of all tension, relieved of what she'd been wanting to say to Annie for weeks, Ruth started to laugh. Becca joined in and together they staggered towards the car, weak with laughter, tears streaming down their cheeks.

When they'd recovered and dried their eyes, Becca asked, 'Where next?'

'The Samaritans.'

Becca suddenly sobered. 'Perhaps I'll give them a miss. They may remember me.'

'I didn't know it ever got that bad,' Ruth said, concerned.

'Oh, it got bad, at one point. It's quite bad now, as a matter of fact.' Ruth reached over and patted her hand. 'Dennis is right, of course. A child can't be expected to carry my load.'

'You can carry it yourself,' Ruth said emphatically. 'Without a drink.'

'How long?' Becca asked bleakly.

'As long as it takes. That's all there is, in the end.'

Ruth started the engine and was about to drive off when they heard the bell ringers begin their practice session in the church. Laughing again, with a touch of hysteria, they drove away.

Charlotte offered Clive an escape from boredom, and a challenge he couldn't resist. Using every ploy in his considerable repertoire – teasing, cajoling, bargaining, diversionary tactics – he got her to eat. One day it was a banana, then a bar of chocolate, then part of the dinner he was unable to finish himself. She would drift into his room around meal time, settle herself into a chair, and try to provoke him. It was his only entertainment. Gradually, her lethargy began to lift.

Charlotte was a product of a kind of upper class squalor Clive had never dreamed of. Her cynicism seemed bottomless, her despair profound. Their conversations consisted mostly of verbal fencing; the harder she tried to shock him, the harder he tried not to show it. At the end of one long afternoon, he watched her bite into the sausage roll he'd given her and felt a small thrill of accomplishment. She flashed him a mischievous grin: 'It's time for that walk I promised you!'

She had more strength than he'd suspected; as they walked down the corridor, she adjusted her pace to his slower one. 'There's a place in Zurich,' she said matter-of-factly, 'where they treat you in a unit that's really a fallout shelter. Everyone wears masks and rubber gloves. They filter the air and give you an arseful of vitamins every morning, and play Beethoven muzak. In the event of nuclear attack you're thrown out on the streets, so the citizens can survive. My father was very keen to dump me there. Personally, I thought the gutter had more to offer.'

'Which gutter?'

'One long oozing gutter from Paris to Edinburgh.' He

reached into the pocket of his dressing gown and handed her another sausage roll. 'Where did you get these?'

'The porter brought them in.' To his satisfaction, she munched away. 'Why here?' he asked.

'I was thrown off a train for scaring the shit out of a load of commuters. They put me into a detox unit. I was "referred" when it dawned on them I'd got something more than withdrawal symptoms.'

'Where are we going?' Clive asked. If it was much further, he'd have to sit down.

'Not too much further.' She walked more slowly, to accommodate him. 'When your wife comes at night, what do you talk about?'

'Nothing much now,' he said equably.

'Is that because she's stupid?'

'It's because we understand one another.'

'She is heavily deluded, your wife,' Charlotte said bitterly. 'You can't do anything about the Plague.'

'There'll be a cure one day,' Clive said without conviction.

Charlotte laughed humourlessly. 'Balls. There's a lot of death around. It's in demand – it's a pop video. What's her exhibition about? Safe sex and clean needles? Someone should tell her the best buzz, the only buzz, is dangerous sex and dirty needles.'

He tried to imagine her, no more than a child, really, sticking a dirty needle into her arm. He shuddered. 'Who gave you the needle first?'

'My mother's coke supplier.'

'My God!'

'It was only like having her woman at St Laurent look after my clothes.'

Her tone chilled him as much as her words. He at least had *had* a life, while Charlotte – he couldn't bear the thought of the waste. 'You can get better than you are, you know,' he said, desperately wanting her to believe it. 'You're better now than you were—'

121

'And what will I do when I'm better?' she scoffed.

'Make a life—'

'Out of what?' They were approaching the entrance to a ward. 'Here we are, Clive.'

'What is this?'

She led him through the doors. 'It's the geriatrics. Ladies here, gentlemen next door. The nurses make jokes about them sleepwalking. Very *déclassé*, nurses.'

Clive found himself gazing at a vision of hell. A dozen or so withered old women sat, some of them in wheelchairs, in what appeared to be a graveyard for the living. One of them looked up: 'Daddy?' she asked expectantly. The others were a collection of useless stick limbs, gaping mouths, vacant eyes, wasted flesh. The smell of urine and disinfectant was overwhelming; Clive tried not to gag. One woman sat on the floor, rocking. Another, attached to an oxygen tank by a plastic pipe in her nose, mumbled unintelligibly to herself. A woman in a wheelchair near the door held her dentures in her lap, weeping soundlessly.

'You come here often?' Clive asked, appalled.

'Yes,' Charlotte said airily. 'It's my promenade.' A nurse administering medication glanced in their direction; Charlotte pulled Clive out of sight. 'Careful, don't let the staff see you. They get furious at our sort – they think we should wear a scarlet A on our foreheads.' She glanced at Clive, enjoying his reaction. 'They're very quiet today, actually. Someone's been round with the Largactil. On better days they rub mashed potatoes in their hair and scream back at *Crossroads*.'

'I'm going,' Clive said weakly. She grabbed his arm. 'No! Look! *That's* what we're missing! I'll never, never be old. Nor, I have to tell you this, Clive, will you.'

'That's enough,' he implored. He started back towards their own ward, as quickly as he could. 'Slow down,' Charlotte said. 'The tour isn't over yet.'

He stopped and leaned against the wall, coughing; when he recovered his breath he asked, 'Why didn't you finish yourself off long ago?'

'I did my best. I OD'd twice. Since I've been off the stuff, I've lost my nerve. However, I'm back in training now.'

Clive felt disoriented; they seemed to be in a little-used section of the vast hospital complex. Charlotte opened an unmarked door and ushered him into a sluice room. She shut the door and leaned against it. 'Alone at last. I found this place one night. No one ever comes here. This is where I'll do it, when I'm ready.'

'Come on,' he said, incredulous.

'It's never crossed your mind?'

'Okay, at first, perhaps—'

'No, Clive – not at first. *Since*. As you get weaker—' He shook his head. 'The only decent thing my brother's ever done for me is send me a box of the brown pills.'

'Pills?'

'There's a health farm in Malta where they dish them out to terminals. No pain, nothing.'

He believed her – and was horrified. 'You're eighteen!'

'Yes.' She gazed at him speculatively. 'Do you know why I latched on to you, Clive? I used to see men like you, nice Englishmen with decent families, on holiday in France, at places where we tied up the boat in summer. I'd sit on deck stoned, and fantasise that someone like you looked after me.'

Clive felt a wave of tremendous tenderness. 'I'll try to look after you,' he said softly.

'Though we'd screw, wouldn't we, if either of us could manage it?'

'No,' he lied.

'Yes,' she said. Again, the speculative gaze. 'It was a girl, wasn't it, with you?'

'Yes.'

She took his hands and whispered, her voice infinitely seductive. 'We can do the next best thing. We can hold hands and go together . . .' Distraught, shaking, he leaned against the sink and looked at her helplessly. 'It'd be easy,' she crooned. 'They'd be glad. Everyone'd be glad. It'd be our choice . . .'

Chapter 15

Preparations for the exhibit filled Ruth's days; she used up the last of her Valium and was too busy to renew the prescription. It was hard work, but satisfying when she began to get results. With only a handful of helpers she had lined up speakers from the medical community, plastered the town with posters announcing the event, persuaded the local media to run free, fair-minded publicity. But despite all her detailed planning, the last-minute activity was frantic. The evening before the opening, the little band of volunteers gathered in the library's community room to tie up any loose ends. Outside, the sign Scott had carefully hand-lettered announced:

> AIDS AND THE COMMUNITY
> AN EXHIBIT PRESENTED BY THE
> LENTONBURY PUBLIC LIBRARY
> WHAT KIND OF PEOPLE GET AIDS?
> PEOPLE WHO DON'T KNOW THE FACTS

Ruth was helping Nell fasten her photographs into place when Dennis walked in, brandishing the evening paper. Ruth looked up, pleased. 'Can't keep away from us, can you?'

'He likes to be where the action is,' Becca said, smiling.

Dennis looked only slightly embarrassed. 'I was just passing by . . . I wondered if you'd read the letters?' He shook the paper open and read, '"I cannot be persuaded that the proposed exhibit meets any aspect of public demand. It is yet another area in which so-called liberal opinion is being allowed more credibility and attention than it deserves. We should protest as forcibly as we know how." That's from a Colonel Dudley Forster, and there's another one from the Chairman of the Rotary Club: "Is This Why Rotarians Support Hospital Charities?"'

Ruth stopped him: 'Don't bother.'

'Are you going to reply?' he asked.

'Why don't you?'

'I *told* you—'

Ruth smiled. 'I know. You won't be associated.'

'Look,' Dennis said placatingly, 'seeing I'm here, I'll give you a hand. But nothing public.'

'How about setting up that display stand?' Ruth asked.

Becca picked up his discarded newspaper. 'What *do* we do about the letters?' she asked.

'Ignore them,' Ruth said firmly.

Across the room, Nell called out 'What about these *French* letters? Do you want to hit the customers with a display at the door?'

If it was a test, Ruth passed with flying colours; she had no time for inhibitions. 'Condoms go on the wall,' she said. Nell grinned. Behind her, Morrie inspected the photograph of himself collapsing over the finishing line in the joy race.

'What's that meant to be? "AIDS Victim Triumphs Over Adversity?" Who'd've given me the kiss of life, then?' he asked Scott flirtatiously.

'Well, it wouldn't've been the St John's Ambulance.'

'I should hope not; there's not a decent kisser among 'em. Hey, Becca!' Morrie called out, 'What did you do with our true confessions?'

'We made a careful selection, on purely literary grounds. The last captions, over there.' She gestured towards a display across the room. Pleased, Morrie walked over to have a look.

Scott spoke confidentially to Ruth. 'He's been spouting

into that tape recorder day and night. Talk about Ernest Hemingway. Just as well. I've been doing a lot of over-time. Thought I'd try and get him across to Italy. Pal of his from the old days rang up and offered us a house. I'd just have to keep him wrapped up on the flight. He's running again, too, properly.'

'He looks good.'

'We've compromised on the macrobiotics. We have brown rice *and* chocolate éclairs.'

Morrie recognised his own words on one of the captions and whooped with delight. 'Listen: "When I'm running, I know that I'm in tune with all the rhythms of my body, and that they're all flowing as they should".'

'You get that out of *Goal* magazine?' Scott asked.

Morrie ignored him. '"I know that this process is healing – that it's showing me how to be well." Told you that was a good bit,' he bragged.

'The rhythms of his body,' Scott said with mock de-rision. 'Who gives them a kick-start every day? I'm glad you knocked out the mighty thunder of his heartbeat, Becca! Hey, I almost forgot – did you get anyone to open this effort yet?'

Becca laughed. 'We've had positive refusals from three gay actors, two MPs, a titled lady and an alternative comedian.'

'The presenter of the television programme was will-ing,' Ruth said, 'but he was already booked. I'm going to ask Dr Singleton.'

From the far corner of the room, Dennis called out, 'Listen, Ruth – it should be you!'

'No, no – of course not,' she said, surprised and flustered.

'He's right,' Scott said, 'of course it should be you, Ruthie! Who better?'

'They're right, Mum,' Nell chimed in.

Ruth laughed, embarrassed to be the centre of

attention. 'Well, we'll . . . I'll see. Look, we'd better get out of here. They'll be locking up the building in a minute.'

'My landlady's got me off the hook till nine,' Dennis said.

Only half-joking, Becca said, 'I'll be suing her for alienation of affection.'

'Aw, come on – you'll see Fraser at the weekend.'

'I know. Sorry. I had a letter from my two this morning. It tends to curdle me for the rest of the day.'

Dennis looked round at the others: 'I could just about set up three halves of lager and a tomato juice.'

Nell, carrying leftover mat boards towards the door, stuck her thumb up to accept. 'Thanks,' Ruth said, 'I'll catch you up.' The others filed out of the door while she collected her coat, handbag and papers. She was on her way out when the tall figure of a man blocked the doorway. 'Bill?' she said, astonished. Stanhope stood there swaying: she realised he was quite drunk. 'What do you want?' she asked. Instead of replying, he walked unsteadily over to the nearest display board, where the photos of Clive and Morrie were mounted. 'What is it, Bill?' she repeated.

'I'm sorry,' he said, slurring his words, 'the company . . .'

'What about the company?' she asked, bewildered.

He drew himself up, a drunk absurdly affecting dignity. 'The company would rather not know that one of its executives contracted a social disease while on company business. It would rather its competitors didn't know, either.'

'I don't understand,' Ruth faltered.

'When the executive's wife starts being visible as a champion of the cause, then the company . . . has to take action.' He gestured helplessly at the exhibition. 'I'm sorry,' he said again. 'Sorry . . .'

*

Hearing the news the next afternoon, Clive was sympathetic but not totally surprised. 'You must have known we wouldn't make it,' Ruth said. She felt shattered. She'd come straight to the hospital from the library, where she'd helped to dismantle the exhibit. It had been like witnessing a small death – all the weeks of planning undone in scarcely an hour.

'I hoped you would,' Clive said fervently. In anticipation of her visit he had forced himself out of bed and into a chair. 'I keep spoiling things for you, don't I?'

'I tried to speak to the library committee . . . the hospital management board . . .'

'Singleton told me.'

'Before he left for his holiday?' Ruth asked. How could the consultant have abandoned them when they needed him most?

'He had to go away, Ruth. He can't afford to stay hopeless in his job.'

'Hopeless?'

'The company chairman's on the hospital management board. So is Martin's MP friend, and on the library committee.'

'Langley . . . of course.' Clive searched for words of comfort but found none. 'Nell's photographs were the best she's ever done,' Ruth said despondently. 'The man she works for gave her a hand. There was so much good will – I think the vicar might even have joined us eventually.'

Clive made an effort: 'It's not the end. You'll go on from here.'

'*Where?*' Ruth asked bitterly. '*Where should I go?*'

From his chair, Clive looked up at his wife, admiration mingled with remorse. 'The pity is we didn't discover what was in you a long time ago.'

'You wouldn't have wanted it then,' Ruth said; unable to deny it, he slumped in his chair, weighed down by regrets. She tried to reassure him: 'I was happy enough.'

'Were you?'

She reflected. 'Well . . . now it seems as though I spent too much time being afraid. Afraid of making mistakes. Afraid of failing you and the children—'

'When really I failed you.'

'Stop it! There's no point. We both chose a certain kind of life . . .'

'We didn't even choose it. It was the kind of life we'd always had.' They shared a long, not uncomfortable silence. 'What now?' Clive said at last.

'I thought I might go away by myself for a few days. To the cottage. Would you mind?' He shook his head. She strained for a positive note. 'Then we might be able to get you home.' They exchanged a look of perfect understanding. She kissed him tenderly and reached for her coat.

Arm in arm, they walked down the corridor to the lift, Clive wheezing but striving not to show his fatigue. With Ruth safely inside the lift, he leaned against the wall for support, coughing violently. Finally, somewhat recovered, he shuffled slowly back to his room, which seemed miles away. He climbed laboriously into bed and lay there staring at the ceiling, filled with desolation.

'Has life lost its meaning yet?' Charlotte asked breezily from the doorway. He began to cough again. She surveyed him intently. 'From the look of you, we'd better make it soon. The brown pills, I mean.' She sauntered in, sat on the edge of his bed and waited for his coughing to subside.

'I thought you were starting to feel better,' he said.

'It won't last. Besides, it's got to be before next Tuesday!'

'Why?'

'They won't keep me here after that.'

Her unexpected announcement was a shock. In spite of the differences in their ages, backgrounds and experience, a curious, intense intimacy had developed between them. She saw him as he was, accepted him as he was; only in her company was he able to contemplate the abyss.

'Where will you go?'

'Nowhere, I told you. I'm not leaving.'

He made a final, feeble effort to dissuade her: 'Look, Ruth found some amazing pockets of good will when she was setting up the exhibition . . .'

'I hope you're not suggesting that I go and live in an amazing pocket of good will,' she scoffed.

'No. You'd soon pollute it.'

Charlotte was not amused. 'I've been all right to you,' she said.

'Only so you'd have someone to talk death at.'

'You know I'm right.'

He couldn't look at her. 'Yes. It'd better be the brown pills then.'

She looked sceptical. 'Do you mean it?'

'Yes,' he said, his voice barely audible.

'Tonight?'

He shrugged, nonchalant. 'If you like.'

Chapter 16

Driving back to her rented townhouse, Ruth felt physically and emotionally drained. She decided to take the train to Norfolk the next morning; perhaps it would recharge her batteries, restore her perspective. She tried not to think about the collective effort that had gone into the exhibit, and the injustice of its closure. How could people in power be so shortsighted, have so little sense of the damage, perhaps even deaths, that continued ignorance and distortion would cause?

Parking the car, she saw a familiar figure waiting on her doorstep. It was Scott. He ran towards her, wildly waving a letter. 'It's Morrie,' he said distraught. 'He's gone!'

Ruth took him inside, sat him at the kitchen table, put the kettle on and tried to calm him. 'What happened?'

'He bust the tapes when he got home last night. I tried to tell him they'd be used sooner or later, but he wasn't having any. Then this morning I caught him looking at himself in the bathroom mirror, going over ever inch. He's got hundreds of them now, little purple lumps.'

'But where's he gone?'

'He didn't say in the note.'

'When?'

'Must've been between ten and eleven. I had to go out – I had a batch of worksheets to post. I wanted him to run there with me, but he wouldn't. He said running's out.'

'You've no idea?'

Her cut her off. 'Yeah, yeah, I've an idea. I *know*, in fact. There's only one place he *would* go.'

'Where?'

Ruth handed him his tea; his voice broke, 'I can't say. I don't want to say . . .'

Ruth sat opposite him and leaned forward. 'What can we do?'

'Nothing,' he said, weeping. 'I shouldn't have come here. You've had enough—'

'If you know where he is—'

'I should leave him there!' Scott burst out angrily. 'I should let him fester! Only . . . Listen, he was into fast lane stuff, I told you. You know what that means?' She nodded, feeling a twinge of apprehension. 'On the uppers and screwing himself soft all night long.'

Ruth drew back. 'He wouldn't—'

'Why not? He's talked about it before, when he's been pissed off. You know, "What's the point, may as well go out for a lay." He doesn't look that ill, not about the face. And in the dark—'

'But he could infect someone!'

'Don't tell *me*! I only love him!' Ruth watched him, feeling helpless and confused. 'He said I was too conscientious,' Scott went on, beside himself, 'but it meant we could fit everything in – his health programme, the relaxation, the running, I liked it. I mean, there was the anxiety, but when it was going smoothly, it was a good way to live. I thought we'd better tell his mother when it happened. She hadn't seen him in years.' He laughed bitterly. 'Came in the front door and said he'd never looked better in his life. Wouldn't believe he was ill! Mind you, that was when the first wave was over . . .'

Wearily, Ruth got to her feet. 'We'd better find him.'

'You can't go in those places!' Scott protested.

'I'll drive you.'

'He won't be there till after dark.'

'We'll wait.'

'I might need some help. He can get fighting mad.'

'We'll get some help.' She reached for the telephone and dialled Dennis's number, hoping he'd be there.

Bill Stanhope sat alone at the golf club bar, drinking moodily while his wife officiously played out her role as a committee member. 'Any more names now, please, for the husband and wife teams? Come on Jack, you can show everyone how you've improved Miriam's game.' She moved to another table. 'Husbands and wives, please! Instant divorce, somebody called it. Thank you, David, dear — are you *sure* Lizzie's going to agree? After last year . . . ?'

All eyes suddenly turned from Annie towards the entrance. Becca stood in the doorway, looking a great deal more self-possessed than she felt. She wore a clinging red jersey dress and red spike heels; her coppery hair was pinned up with two filigreed silver combs. Enjoying the ripple of interest, she strode purposefully towards Stanhope, seated herself beside him and nodded to the barman. He handed her a glass of tomato juice. 'What are you doing, Bill?' she asked.

He gazed at her blearily. 'What does it look like?'

'It looks unwise. You don't want to end up like me, do you?'

'You look fine, Becca,' he said approvingly. 'Absolutely terrific.'

'You can't see the cracks from where you're standing,' she murmured.

'Listen,' he said raising his glass: 'I'm celebrating!'

'No, really?' Becca said with mock surprise.

'I've been promoted.'

Becca's voice, always husky, grated like glasspaper. 'Oh? I didn't know they had grades of doctor. What are you now, chest sounder to the MD?'

'They call it Company Health Adviser. It's worth ten thousand a year more.'

'Good. You can extend the swimming pool and keep a couple of Filipinos.'

He forced a laugh. Annie, ever vigilant, left her table and joined them. 'This is a rare pleasure,' she said icily. Bill stared meditatively into his glass, and Becca raised her eyebrows. 'I mean, considering you were so anxious to remain a member, it's surprising we don't see more of you.'

Only sobriety prevented Becca from pouring her drink down the front of Annie's dress. 'Until just last night,' she said pointedly, 'I was pretty busy with other activities.'

'I heard,' Annie smirked.

'Then surely you'll have heard they've come to a sudden end.'

'I can't find it in my heart to be sorry if that ... *unwelcome* exhibition has been cancelled.'

'What *can* you find it in your heart to be?' Becca purred. 'Anyway it's postponed, not cancelled.' She glanced at Bill. 'One advantage of being tipped off was that at least we could do our own face-saving before the big guns arrived.'

Annie looked at Bill suspiciously. 'Public opinion was against you.'

'Well-mobilised, I'd say. What do *you* get out of it, Annie? A Queen's Award for Industry? Or did you just add an MP to your guest list?'

'If you'll excuse me,' Annie sniffed, 'I have committee business.'

'Don't go on my account. I'm only here to ask Bill if he'll do something for me. Something *else*, I mean.'

Reluctantly, Bill looked up from his glass. 'Yes?'

'Well, you know how it is when you see some really abject piece of shittiness happen? You can either drown in it or, with a bit of effort, you can crank yourself into rising above it. Somewhat to my surprise, I seem to be cranking.'

'And?'

'I'm going to reapply for custody of my children. I have to find people who'll testify to my suitability.'

Annie froze. Bill put his glass down on the bar, cleared his throat and, for the first time, spoke decisively. 'Would a Company Health Adviser do?'

Becca smiled. 'Admirably.'

'Good.'

'Thanks.' Becca leaned forward and gave Bill a chaste, grateful kiss on the mouth. She turned to Annie: 'That's my second kiss today. I've been to see Clive in the hospital. I kissed him, too. Just before I came here.' Becca gave herself a moment to enjoy the sight of speechless, stupefied Annie – then turned and, with real confidence now, swept out of the club.

Ruth's gloved hand gripped the steering wheel tightly as the car crawled through the littered, rain-slick streets of a world she had never imagined. 'Used to be a lot more crowded down here,' Scott said. 'Couldn't find a parking place to save your life. Now it's dropping off. Only silly buggers like Morrie keep them going.' Each time he got out of the car to investigate another establishment, Ruth peered into the shadows, fear mingling with fascination. Men in doorways, lounging on steps, leaning against buildings, leered at her. Heavily made-up women appraised her with hard eyes; was she buying or selling? Hunters and hunted, she thought. A market of flesh. Some of the clubs were lit up with garish neon signs; others were inconspicuous black holes in black walls.

She and Dennis had been waiting for at least five minutes outside a place identified as NIGHTHAWKS – MEMBERS ONLY. 'You can't have seen much of this before,' he remarked.

'Have you?'

'You must be joking!' He looked out the window with

distaste. 'It's all money . . . whatever you can afford. Like anything else – they go in for overstimulating an appetite, then they cash in on feeding it.'

'You disapprove of the appetite, of course.'

'I disapprove of the appetite for three cars and all.'

'My family had three cars . . .'

Dennis backed off. 'Aw, jeez, let's drop it. Even to me I sound like a Sunday School teacher.'

Scott ran up to the car window. 'He's in there! Someone got a good look at him and sent for the police!' Dennis quickly got out of the car and followed Scott back into the club. Ruth sat in the car for a moment; a passer-by shot her a curious look and said something she didn't quite catch. Impelled by a curiosity of her own, she too got out of the car and followed the men inside.

The music hit her first – the whole building reverberated to the thudding, deafening rock beat. The air was thick with smoke and the smell of perspiring bodies. Strobe lights flashed intense red and blue lights on the centre of the room, where a blur of glistening white skin, leather, denim, punk slashes and chains moved in time with primeval rhythms, like a grotesque travesty of the hotel ballroom. She stood transfixed, the object of unmistakably hostile stares; she felt an electrical charge in the air.

Morrie stood at the bar wearing vest, leather jacket and jeans, his back turned to the approaching Scott. His lover touched his shoulder: 'Are you coming?'

Morrie angrily shook him off and whirled to face him. 'Where's your uniform?' he sneered, very drunk.

Scott spoke urgently: 'Let's go.'

'No. Listen: it's got to be the starched hat and the white pinny . . .'

Scott grabbed his arm: 'We're moving.'

Violently, Morrie shook him off. 'Sorry! I've got another engagement. He's just gone to the bog, but he'll

137

be back in a minute.' Scott nodded at Dennis and, together, they began hustling a violently resisting Morrie towards the door. Dennis saw Ruth, and momentarily lost his grip on Morrie. 'Bloody hell!' he exploded. 'Get out of here!'

Outside, a police car was waiting; the three policemen standing beside it watched as Morrie landed a blow to Scott's ear. 'Going to give us a hand, then?' Scott yelled, furious.

'You look as if you're doing all right,' an officer said. Morrie made a lunge for freedom and all three policemen scattered, as though in fear of their lives. With a coordinated burst of strength, Scott and Dennis grabbed Morrie and shoved him, still struggling, into the back seat of the car. They got in beside him as Ruth, already in the driver's seat, started the engine – and flooded it.

'Shit-face!' Morrie screamed at Scott. 'Arsehole! I'm getting out of here!' He rammed an elbow into Scott's side.

Scott gasped for breath. 'You're staying—'

'Not with you, you shit-faced ponce! You fucking granny! Granny . . .'

Scott was livid. 'Shut it will you!'

'You shut it, granny! Done the fucking ironing today? Rinsed your smalls out? Had your sodding meditation?'

'I'll kill you,' Scott said, drawing back his fist.

'Yeah? Come on, come on, then! Give us a heave, out of this—' he fought to get to the door handle. 'Come on, arsehole.'

Grim-faced and desperate, Dennis suddenly turned and clipped Morrie hard on the jaw. The engine started at last. Narrowly missing one of the policemen, Ruth drove away.

Chapter 17

Propped up on pillows in his bed, Clive was laboriously writing a last letter to his wife. It was proving even more difficult than he'd anticipated; frustrated, he crumpled a sheet of paper and began again. 'I can't ask you to forgive me, but I hope you will understand my desire to get this over with as quickly as possible, for your sake and the children's as well as my own. I've caused all of you so much pain already—' He was interrupted by a knock at the door. 'Aren't you a bit overeager?' he called out. The door opened and he looked up, expecting to see Charlotte. Instead, Bill Stanhope, looking absolutely terrified, walked into the room.

'The night sister said five minutes,' Bill said apprehensively, 'but I'll leave, if you'd rather.'

Wheezing, Clive motioned him to a chair. Both Ruth and Becca had mentioned that the company doctor had been drinking heavily of late, but he appeared to be stone cold sober at the moment. Sober, but tormented. He leaned forward and spoke with emotion. 'I just had to tell you, Clive, how terribly sorry I am about . . . everything. I could give you a carload of excuses for the way I behaved, but the real reason was simply cowardice. I'm sorry, and I wanted to tell you so.'

Clive felt he was seeing Stanhope through the wrong end of a telescope – sharply defined, but very far away. What did Stanhope want from him? Forgiveness? 'You did what anyone else would have done in your position,' he said.

Stanhope shook his head. 'Not *anyone* else.'

Clive couldn't absolve him, but he did understand. 'Well, pragmatism's a sound management technique. Go for the interests of the group. I've pulled fast deals in the past, lost men their jobs. Decent men.'

'I'm not cut out for company work,' Stanhope said despondently. 'I realise that now.'

'You'd be a fool to leave.'

Stanhope laughed bitterly: 'I couldn't pay the mortgage either.'

'Well, that's a perfectly practical consideration.'

'I could lower my mortgage,' he said, continuing the argument that had been going on in his head for weeks.

'Most people don't. People like us.'

'Is that the bottom line, then?'

'So it seems.' The coughing began again.

Stanhope contemplated Clive's ravaged face in dismay. 'Is there anything I can do for you? Or Ruth?'

'No,' Clive said wheezing. 'Perhaps afterwards . . .'

'Afterwards?'

'I can't have very long.'

Stanhope stood up. 'When I told her the company was going to get the exhibition closed, she was so afraid it might be the last straw for you – that you wouldn't want to go on living . . .'

Clive looked at him sharply, feeling a sudden resolution of his inner turmoil. Charlotte's answer was the wrong answer – for both of them. Whatever mistakes he'd made, he was going to get his last act right. 'There *is* something you can do for me,' he said. 'There's a girl here . . . she's only eighteen . . . she thinks she has no future. Her name is Charlotte. She has a great spirit, a lot of potential – but she's on a death kick. She's in remission. It could last years, but she needs . . . to be looked after. A place to stay . . .'

A half-hour later, the two men were deep in con-

140

versation when Charlotte appeared in the doorway – barefoot, her eyes unnaturally bright. 'Shall I come back later?' she asked.

'Have a seat,' Clive said. She perched on the end of his bed. 'This is Dr Stanhope. We've been talking about you. Have you any A-levels?'

'What?' she asked, bewildered.

'Have you got any A-levels?'

She flashed him a look of disgust. 'Even at death's door, you're still riddled with British middle-class obsessions.'

'*Have* you?' Stanhope asked.

'No. I have the International Baccalaureat. With A's in all subjects. What has that got to do with anything?'

Clive shifted his position and waited for another bout of coughing to subside. 'Dr Stanhope has a proposition for you.'

She glanced quickly from Clive to Bill, and back again.

'Do you know anything about Quakers?' the doctor asked.

'I understand they're lousy conversationalists.' She hopped down from the bed. 'Look, I'll come back in a while.'

'Sit down,' Clive said. 'There's been a change in plans. Bill here knows some Quakers who run a market garden in the Cotswolds. he thinks you could stay with them for a while . . . for some breathing space. Until you feel stronger—'

'You mean I could do Open University credits and grow cabbages in an air of religious calm? No, thank you.'

With surprising energy, Clive leaned forward and grabbed her shoulders. 'Listen to me! You're not going to die! You're going to live for as long as you can, right at the top of your ability. You'll get help. I promise you – Bill will see to it. Other people will help. You've got to live for a cure. You've got to let them try to cure you so they'll know when they've got it right. Not just for you but for other people, and perhaps not just for what you've got. You've got to make what use you can of yourself, until the very last minute!'

With Stanhope looking on, dumbstruck, Charlotte began to cry. 'And what about you?'

Clive only hesitated for an instant. 'Me, too. I might get out before long.'

'You won't.' she sobbed.

'I recovered before . . .' he said weakly. He sank back on his pillows, exhausted. Stanhope put an arm around Charlotte and led her towards the door. 'Come on, Charlotte,' he said gently. 'I'll walk you home.'

Ruth waited in her car outside Scott's flat while Dennis and Scott unloaded a repentant Morrie and helped him into the building. She saw Scott appear in a lighted window, then disappear as he drew the curtains shut. She closed her eyes and rested her head on the steering wheel, wondering how she would find the energy to drive home. Dennis tapped on the car window: 'Want me to drive?' She nodded, moved wearily into the passenger seat and tried to switch her mind off.

Images, sounds, colours flashed through her brain like the strobe lights in the club. She was confused, shaken, tense – her whole body felt like a clenched fist. Dennis looked shaken, as well. 'Better come in for a drink', she said. Wordlessly he followed her into the townhouse. She threw off her coat, got out the cognac and poured each of them a generous shot. 'Seen this?' Dennis asked. He pointed to a message inscribed in lipstick on the mirror over the fireplace: STAYING OVER AT NICKY'S – SEE YOU MORNING – NELL X

Ruth sighed. 'Nicky.'

'The boyfriend?'

'Her employer, technically. A Cockney lad.' She laughed ironically. 'We'd probably have called him "unsuitable" once.'

'What do you call him now?'

'A godsend.' She handed him his glass. He sat, only slightly uncomfortable, in a straight-backed chair, watching Ruth carefully. 'Some night, eh?'

The brandy warmed Ruth, but the tension tightened. 'I don't know how to . . . how to deal with it,' she said.

'You dealt with it okay.' He spoke so softly she could scarcely hear him.

'No.' She shook her head vehemently. 'I mean now. What it means. I mean, thinking, sitting outside those places, watching people go in there. Drawn in . . . Morrie in that state, and Scott loving him. The desperation. The fear. *My* fear.' Dennis rose and walked slowly towards her; unheeding, she went on, trembling, words spilling out, on the edge of hysteria. 'And Clive . . . thinking of Clive, and what he knew about that – not about *men*, especially, I mean women, too, whatever it was that happened. That excitement and that danger . . . that *passion* that even my own daughter knows about at some level, and I *don't*. I *don't*! I *don't*!'

Drawn by her need as much as his own, Dennis touched her cheek. 'Is this what you mean?' he whispered hoarsely. 'Is it?' He stroked her neck; his hand moved to her breast. 'Is it? Is this what you want?' Ruth caught the faint scent of the nightclub – the smoke, the sweat, the alcohol. Feeling giddy, defenceless, but knowing exactly what she was doing, she drew him to her and kissed him, surrendering to sensations that sent her spinning finally, totally, blessedly out of control.

Chapter 18

In her parents' house, at boarding school, in her own home with Clive and the children, Ruth had always adjusted without question to other people's rhythms, demands, expectations. Norfolk promised solitude; she wondered what it would be like.

It wasn't true solitude, though; the cottage was crowded with memories. Was it perversity that caused her to remember only happy times? Had there really been no bad ones? She recalled Martin waking them all in the middle of the night, when a stray cat had wandered into his room to deliver a litter; Nell nursing an injured bird back to health; Clive fly-fishing for their supper, splitting logs for the fire; the long summer days of walks and picnics; picking berries, building sand castles; puzzles and games on rainy afternoons; evenings at the local pub, where they'd celebrated birthdays, anniversaries, promotions. On these roads, she and Clive had bicycled, each with a child perched in a wobbly front seat. On these roads, he'd helped her to conquer her fear of driving a car. In retrospect, it all seemed impossibly idyllic. The cottage had been a refuge from reality. Now she'd come here to face reality. Where had it all gone wrong?

It hadn't *all* gone wrong, surely. That the sex had never been right was clear enough to her now, but how could she possibly have known that when the knowledge might have been of some use? How can you miss what you've never experienced? If her knowledge of Clive had been shallow, had she known herself any better? Certainly the woman who had moaned with pleasure on the hearthrug in the townhouse was a Ruth she'd never dreamed existed.

She scarcely thought of Dennis, and felt no guilt; what had happened between them seemed, in hindsight, as inevitable as the tide. She spent hours on the beach each day, bundled up against the damp salt air. The sea had always soothed her; now it gave her a heightened sense of continuity, a promise that however stormy its surface, in its still, silent depths there was peace. She dreamed of a faceless man who made love to her with all Dennis' passion. She knew it was Clive. She felt an ineffable sadness – and she felt intensely, achingly alive.

'My dearest Clive,' she wrote on the third day. 'I left everything behind me, even the car, and have walked and thought and slept and eaten at a pace that has been, I suppose, truly mine for the first time in my life. Think, I've never been alone before for longer than a day. And the strange thing is, I'm not afraid. Losing fear is something, isn't it? Though I wish with all my heart that it could have happened some other way.

'It was so hard at first to see life going on, ordinary workday life all around, and not feel singled out in some terrible way. Why us? I keep thinking of your loneliness, your isolation, and how you've lived through it all these weeks without making it a burden to me.

'What is there to say about us? Do I still love you in spite of everything? Could I ever have loved you when I didn't know you completely? I can't answer. I do know that the person I am now is full of admiration and regard for the person you've become as a result of all this. And nothing you did has spoiled what was really good about our lives before. It adds up to some kind of love, doesn't it? At any rate, I want you to know that if you need my forgiveness in any formal sense, you have it.

'No more Good Works, though. Dr Singleton wrote to

say that we should see the closing of the exhibition as a temporary setback, but what energy I have is for you. It's the very least I can give you, after all you've given me . . .'

Clive fought the impulse to weep when he read Ruth's letter. Charlotte would be leaving the hospital in a few minutes, and he wanted to see her off with a bit of panache. He had dressed for the occasion in his street clothes, now several sizes too large, but his right arm wasn't working properly and the effort of tying his tie was proving unaccountably difficult. He was leaning heavily against the chest of drawers in his room, coughing, when Charlotte appeared in the doorway. It was the first time he'd seen her in anything but the blue silk kimono. She looked striking in a stylishly cut long grey woollen dress, pointed black leather boots and an enormous floppy brown hat with two long feathers. 'Clive!' she admonished him, 'you shouldn't have dressed!' She went to him and with casual intimacy, expertly knotted his tie.

'Oh, one has to keep up standards,' he said, wheezing.

She twirled around playfully. 'This is last season's, I'm afraid.'

'You look fine.'

'Pretty effective way to shift the puppy fat, eh?' Her eyes were bright with bravado, her cynicism transparent as glass. She looked so terribly young and vulnerable – he had to get her out quickly, otherwise he'd break down. 'Aren't they waiting for you downstairs?' he asked, and began to usher her into the corridor. 'Oh . . . Bill Stanhope says he'll be looking in on you from time to time—'

'Ah, yes. The repentant company doctor.'

'And I'll see you myself, as soon as I'm out.'

She rolled her eyes in disbelief. 'Okay.' In the corridor she stopped, surprised to see a group of nurses and patients who had gathered to see her off. 'Oh, come on,' she said, touched but determined not to show it. 'Not a farewell committee. I was never exactly top of the charts.'

Clive took his cue from her: 'It's relief and gratitude. Now we'll all get some sleep.' One of the nurses handed Clive a bouquet that he'd ordered. 'Here. The porter ordered it and brought it in this morning. It's Luton FC colours, I'm afraid.'

Too moved to speak, she practically wrenched the flowers from his hands, kissed him swiftly and set off down the corridor. She called out 'Ciao', but didn't look back.

Singleton emerged from the examination room and called after her. 'Goodbye, Charlotte. See you at checkup time. If you need us before, we're here, remember.' She raised her hand, wriggled her fingers and disappeared into the lift.

Singleton walked back to Clive. 'I had a letter from your wife this morning.'

'So did I.'

'I'm sorry about what happened. I'm just no match for those particular vested interests. Nor for what calls itself public opinion around here. In my specialty, it's usually a matter of proceeding by stealth. I'm grateful for what she was able to do.'

'Give her time.'

'There isn't any time. The clinics are filling up. I don't know who's worse – the fools who get exhibitions closed or the fools who risk infection and go back for more.'

Clive gazed out of the window, feeling bereft, 'There she goes.' They saw a middle-aged couple guiding Charlotte towards a waiting car. She turned, waved up at him . . . and was gone.

'You did a good job with her,' Singleton said.

'What are the chances?'

'The chances are she'll be back on heroin in two

months. Still, the chances are always being confounded in this job. I keep being rescued from cynicism just in the nick of time.' He appraised Clive shrewdly. 'What's wrong with your arm?'

'Nothing . . . except that I can't move it. The leg isn't too cooperative, either.'

'Back to bed,' Singleton ordered.

Clive kept his tone light. 'Will I last until Thursday?'

'What's special about Thursday?'

'Ruth's coming home. I don't want her recalled before then.'

Singleton motioned for a nurse to help Clive back to his room. 'Guaranteed,' he promised.

Annie and Bill Stanhope had stopped rowing, but only because they had practically stopped speaking to each other. The harder Annie pushed, the further Bill retreated. For the first time in their thirty years of marriage, she couldn't predict or understand his behaviour. He didn't argue, he didn't defy her he just seemed terrifyingly indifferent.

On the golf course, for example: during the husbands-and-wives competition, he went through the motions of the game almost disdainfully, as though he didn't care. 'You might at least make an effort,' Annie said after he made a particularly listless shot.

'I agreed to take part. That's got to be enough.'

She lined up her own shot and swung, missing the ball completely. 'I don't expect to *win*. We're not the best husband and wife team in the club. I just don't want people thinking there's something wrong because you're playing so atrociously.' She swung again, viciously; the ball sailed towards the green.

'Sorry,' Bill said, as they walked towards his ball. 'It's my concentration.'

'All right, so you went to see Clive. You agreed to help

that girl. I feel squeamish, but I'm not making trouble about it.'

'It would be all the same if you were,' he said .diffidently.

'I just want it to be a secret, that's all. Is that unreasonable?'

'No.'

'At least you've stopped drinking. It was being noticed, you know. People were asking me if you were depressed. I said, "Depressed? He's on top of the world! He loves his job and he's bloody good at it! It's what we always wanted!" Now . . . I don't know what to say. I don't know what you want me to do. Are you still looking for another job?'

'I've told you – I've got a commitment now, close to home.'

'That girl.'

'She has a name. Charlotte.'

'I don't want to hear about her. And you know what will happen if it should get out—'

'I'm not planning to tell anyone, and I don't imagine that you will.'

They reached his ball; he made another mediocre shot and they proceeded towards Annie's ball. 'We're finished,' she said tonelessly, not looking at him. 'Aren't we? This business has finished us.'

'Not necessarily,' he hedged.

'Yes, it has,' she said bleakly. 'He's infected us too. He's poisoned us . . .'

'Well, he's made us think.'

She lined up her shot and swung. They watched the ball soar into the air, veer to the left and land in the rough. 'I don't *want* to think,' she whimpered. 'Why should I have to? I was happy before this. *We* were happy . . . Weren't we?'

'I never considered it,' Bill said.

'And now?'

He merely shook his head, and moved on.

The week in Norfolk gave Ruth the rest she desperately needed, and restored her equilibrium. Closing up the cottage, she braced herself for whatever was to come. If she'd survived the past few months, she told herself, surely she could survive anything. But the worst was yet to come.

The unexpected sight of Becca awaiting her on the station platform made her only slightly apprehensive. She put on a cheerful face: 'What a surprise! I didn't expect to see you! Have you brought the car? I missed it in a way, but not driving was wonderful.' She registered Becca's grave expression and said, 'Let's go straight to the hospital.'

Becca said, 'Nell sent Martin a cable. She's at home, waiting for him.'

Ruth's heart was pounding; on the way to the hospital, with Becca driving at breakneck speed, she feared the worst. 'Why didn't they let me know?'

'Dr Singleton wasn't alarmed until yesterday,' Becca said. 'It's a secondary infection. He says it's fairly common in cases like Clive's.' They hastened from car park to entrance to lift; Becca left her at the door to Clive's room. She paused for a moment, then went inside.

During Ruth's brief absence, Clive's deterioration had been dramatic. He lay in the bed, eyes closed, wan and shrunken, breathing with great difficulty. Resolutely, Ruth put her own feelings aside. Clive's feelings were what mattered now. She composed herself and sat beside his bed. After a moment he opened his eyes and managed a weak smile. 'Hello,' she said softly.

'Hello,' he whispered hoarsely. 'Sorry . . .' She shook her head. 'How was Norfolk?'

'Peaceful. Did you get my letter?'

'Yes. Thanks.' She took his hand. He looked up at a

photograph of the cottage on the wall opposite. 'Nell brought it . . . She's a clever girl'

'Did you tell her that?'

He nodded. 'I never gave her credit before, did I? It was always Martin.'

'We have two clever, decent children.'

'I know. We got that part right, at least.'

'Not just that part.'

'No, not just that.' He struggled to speak. 'Ruth, is there anything . . . anything we haven't talked about that you want to know?'

'No,' she answered with certainty. 'Nothing.'

'About me? About *this*? Anything you want to ask?' She saw a terrible pleading urgency in his eyes. Instinctively, she stood up, slipped off her shoes and climbed onto the bed beside him. 'Shhh,' she said, as though to a frightened child. With infinite tenderness, she lifted his head onto her breast and put her arms around him. 'We don't need to say any more to one another. It's all right, Clive. It's all, all right.'

Gradually, gratefully he relaxed. She continued to hold him until he slept, then crept quietly out of the room, Singleton was in the corridor, waiting for her. He was struck by an indefinable change in her; she looked drawn and anxious, but softer somehow, and stronger, as well. 'The nurse brought a message,' he said. 'Your son's home.'

'I'll go and get him.'

'No – go home and see him. I doubt if there'll be any significant change tonight.'

'When will there be significant change?'

'I don't know.'

'Days? Not longer,' she beseeched him. 'Not weeks. . . ? Please, not weeks.'

The consultant spoke gently: 'I wouldn't think so.'

'Remember what you said that first day?' Ruth asked.

'That we'd never have anything worse to face than knowing he had the disease?' He nodded. 'This is worse.'

'I'm sorry. Most people go through the whole thing in a kind of dream. It's been different for you – better *and* worse.'

'Yes . . .' she said, faintly. Drawing on resources she'd never dreamed she had, Ruth walked steadily down the corridor to find Becca.

Nell poured coffee for Martin, both of them feeling slightly ill at ease after his absence. 'How was your flight?'

'I don't remember.'

'Hong Kong okay?'

'Tolerable. It's not the City.'

'Well, they have such lousy tailors . . .'

Martin frowned; he was in no mood for jokes. 'How are they?'

'They're wonderful together. I don't know what's happened to them. Especially to her.'

He stroked his chin thoughtfully. 'How was it when she was doing all that stuff?'

'What stuff?'

'Spreading the word.'

She tensed at the hint of sarcasm in his voice. 'It was fine, Martin.'

'Sorry. I never did adjust as well as you.'

'You had your moments – dishing your own chances of being our newest Tory hopeful—'

'Yes, well . . . the game was up then, wasn't it?'

'Do I hear a note of regret?'

'I just don't feel that brave coming back here.'

'I shouldn't think it'll be for long.'

The unadorned statement of what was happening gave him pause. 'Poor Dad . . .' was all he could say. She poured more coffee. Martin looked more closely at his

152

surroundings. 'Have you talked about what she'll do afterwards?'

'No.'

'The lease on this place is renewable monthly. She should be encouraged to go back to the other house.'

Nell tried to enlighten him. 'You don't understand. She won't be "encouraged" to do anything now. She's not the same. Anyway, that house is too big for her.'

'Will you be moving out, then?' he asked, just a bit too quickly.

She snapped at him: 'I have no plans! For God's sake, Martin, we're waiting for someone to die!'

'Isn't that Scott? And Morrie?' Ruth asked Becca. It was the first thing she'd said since they left the hospital. Becca had simply driven the car, respecting her silence. She pulled over, just ahead of the two joggers in track suits on the footpath. Scott reached the car first. 'You must be telepathic. I said we'll have to be looking Ruthie up. You got our card?'

Ruth nodded. He looked affectionately over at Morrie, shaking a stone out of his shoe a few metres away. 'Get a load of that tan, eh? Did him a world of good. And no going off the rails or anything. Just a bit of a flirt with the gondoliers.' He shot her a searching look. 'You okay?'

Ruth couldn't speak. 'It's Clive,' Becca said.

Scott's eyes widened. 'Is he bad?'

'Yes.'

'Oh, Jesus Christ,' he sputtered, 'don't tell *him*!' He watched, panicked, as Morrie approached them. 'Don't say a word, please. He can't take it. I've only just got him back on the routine, y'see. I'm sorry and that . . . he's only a kid.'

'It's all right,' Ruth said. 'I understand.'

'I'll try and see you one day, if I can get out alone . . .'

'Don't worry.'

153

Morrie trotted up. 'Hiya.' He gave Scott a flirtatious look. 'Has he been giving you his gondolier story?'

'They only stopped to say hello,' Scott interjected. 'They're in a rush.'

'How's things?' Morrie asked amiably.

He did look well, Ruth thought, involuntarily contrasting his tanned, healthy face with Clive's skeletal one. She said, 'My son's home.'

'From Hong Kong? That's nice.'

'Yeah,' Scott said uneasily.

Becca said, 'We'd better get going.'

'Okay,' Morrie said. 'See you. Come and have a macrobiotic pasta with us some time, Ruth.'

She smiled weakly and he trotted back onto the footpath. 'I'll be thinking about you,' Scott said. 'Terrible, this, isn't it? Loving. . . ?'

Becca dropped Ruth off, declining an invitation to tea; this seemed to be a time for Ruth to be alone with her children. She took the long way home, in order to pass by the playground where Dennis occasionally took Fraser. Her mood lightened when she saw the child, sporting a bright red muffler and hat, vigorously riding a swing. Seeing her, in the thin November sunshine, he smiled broadly and waved. She walked over to where Dennis stood watching his son. 'I've just been with Ruth,' she said. 'Clive's very bad. It's a difficult time for her.'

'What you telling *me* for?' he asked angrily.

'Dennis!' she said startled.

'Oh shite, don't give me that "Dennis" crap!'

'I only meant . . . she can use all the support she can get.'

'Aye, well . . . I've got enough to do.'

'I know,' she said, baffled by his hostility, 'but you and Ruth—'

'Me and Ruth *what*?'

'—and me,' she went on, 'and the gay boys. We've shared a few hard times . . .'

'Did she say to tell me?'

'No, of course not!'

'Right.'

'So you won't go and see her?'

'Ah, leave out the alky therapy,' he snapped. 'You can't always help one another get over things.'

'I thought you had a soft spot for her,' she said innocently.

He turned on her, furious. 'Piss off, will you! Just get lost!' He shouted over to Fraser, still swinging. 'Come on, you! We're getting our tea!'

Becca backed off from whatever she had unintentionally stirred up. 'Fraser looks well,' she said.

'He's fine.'

'The landlady still doing her stuff?'

'It's working out. She sees to him after school.'

'How about school?'

'He's doing great. Gold stars, the lot.'

'I knew it.'

Together, they watched Fraser hop off the swing and steal a quick whirl on the roundabout. 'Get a move on,' his father called.

Becca couldn't resist telling Dennis what was uppermost in her mind. 'The lawyers put in my application for return of custody yesterday.'

'Oh, aye?'

'With a pile of testimonials to say I've been dry for three months.'

He softened slightly. 'I hope it happens, Becca.'

'Thanks.'

She started back towards her car. Dennis called after her: 'You can say I was asking for her.'

Chapter 19

During the next few days, Clive's condition worsened with what he found to be agonising slowness. He was conscious, but too weak to eat, or even to speak; the coughing fits took all his strength. Ruth and the children sat with him, sometimes together, usually in shifts. *How much longer?*, they wondered as he gasped for each breath. He wondered, too.

Charlotte leaned against the poplar tree at the edge of the green space on the grounds of the vast hospital complex, watching a window on the fourth floor, waiting for Ruth to leave. She had to see Clive alone. Not for long, but alone. The little pocket-size park had been the site of the fête; on these footpaths, Morrie had trained for the race. The green lawn was dotted with late-blooming chrysanthemums, yellow puffballs that belied the season. It would have been quite a pleasant spot, but for the ugly grey monolith of a building in which Charlotte knew all too well what was going on.

After an hour-and-a-half, she saw Ruth emerge from the building and walk wearily towards the car park. Charlotte went to the back entrance and made her way through the familiar passageways, up the familiar stairs. Peering through the window in a door at the end of Clive's corridor, she saw a nurse come out of Clive's room and, with another nurse, wheel a food trolley in the direction of the day room. Stealthily, she darted into Clive's room and closed the door. 'Under-staffing in the National Health Service has its uses, Clive,' she whispered.

He didn't hear her; the sound of his laboured breathing strengthened her resolve. She walked to the bed, bent over him and said in a slightly louder whisper, 'Clive? I've come back for you.'

He opened his eyes and looked at her vaguely, disorientated; for an instant he thought she was the girl in New York. Linda – the name drifted, unbidden, into his consciousness. Lately he'd felt twinges of pity for Linda. 'It's Charlotte,' she said. She wore her 'going-away' outfit, and the hat with the defiant feathers. 'Sorry, you're not dead yet. Though I suppose hell could be one continuous dose of me.' She looked at his wasted face. 'What are they doing to you? Not enough, by the look of things. You should've been finished off by now.'

He made an effort to speak. She waited. 'It was my turn to visit you,' he said haltingly, thinking how very happy he was to see her.

'It doesn't matter. I didn't *believe* you about getting better. I've seen enough incipient corpses on the ends of needles to know where *you* were.'

He smiled sardonically. 'Have some respect for the nearly dead.' She laughed. 'Quakers okay?'

'Not bad. Quite a reasonable little pocket of good will, not unduly wholesome. And the penitent doctor came with some article out of *The Lancet* that says a cure may be on the horizon. He'll have to do better than that, though . . . won't he?' She reached for the dressing gown that lay on the end of the bed. 'Now: you're going to sit up and put this on.'

He tried to laugh, but wheezed instead. 'Can't . . .'

'Yes you can.' She pulled him into a sitting position and draped the dressing gown over his shoulders. 'I'm not having you done for indecent exposure before we're through.'

'Where?' he gasped.

'As far as we get. Listen: remember the back way to the

157

geriatrics? There's a wheelchair near the door. It's not far from the lift. Remember?' She swung his legs over the side of the bed and left him there, swaying, while she looked out of the door. She could hear nurses serving meals in the day room. The corridor was deserted.

She half-carried, half-dragged Clive to the lift; she had enough adrenalin for both of them. The door opened; she lowered him to a sitting position on the floor, got in beside him and pushed the button that said 'G'. 'I think the brown pills might've been better, myself,' she said. 'For both of us.'

'No,' he protested.

'Okay, okay.' The door opened; she carried and dragged him down another corridor, this time to an empty wheelchair. 'Into your pram, Clive,' she giggled. He giggled too, liking the idea, amenable to anything, so long as she was with him. She settled him into the chair, unbarred the exit door and wheeled him outside. 'All part of the Plague Pal service.'

He felt a surge of energy. 'What are we going to do?'

'We're going to run,' she said conspiratorially. 'We're going to run out the last bit of your breath. You don't want to hang around any longer, do you?'

He shook his head, grinning, caught up in her wild exuberance. She pushed the chair down a slight incline, towards the grass; it picked up speed. Her hat flew off; her hair streamed behind her as they whizzed along. 'When they had the Plague, in the old days,' she shouted euphorically, 'you know what they did? They danced! Danced till they dropped!' She stopped the chair at the edge of the grass and pulled him to his feet, shaking him. 'It can't take long, Clive! Come *on*!'

Singleton, alerted by the nurse who'd found Clive's bed empty, reached the hospital steps just in time to watch with horrified disbelief as Clive took a few halting steps. His robe fell to the ground; he staggered forward in his pyjamas, then stood unsteadily for a moment, looking up at the sky. With an expression of what Singleton later described to Ruth as rapture on his face he tottered forward, reached out his arms as though embracing his death . . and collapsed on the grass.

As though at an invisible signal, Singleton and a few other onlookers – orderlies and nurses – who had started towards Clive stood back as Charlotte approached the motionless body. She dropped to her knees beside it and gently lifted Clive's head into her lap. She sat there, lovingly stroking his hair, her tears falling on his face.

Chapter 20

Every time Ruth thought she simply had no more grief to dole out, another wave hit her. She stood outside the crematorium in the early morning rain, gazing into the hearse at the spray of white flowers that lay atop the coffin. Other than Nell, Martin, Becca and the vicar, not a soul was in sight. *It's like a macabre version of the anniversary party,* she thought, *only this time not even Becca could save the day.* The vicar was saying something about a memorial service. '... Perhaps ... later ... in church.' She clutched Martin's arm and nodded doubtfully.

One of the undertaker's men motioned the vicar aside. Another car drew up; Bill Stanhope got out, approached Ruth and awkwardly expressed his condolences. Scott came walking hurriedly up the drive and hugged her warmly. 'Morrie couldn't face it,' he said. 'He says he's sorry.'

'Tell him it's all right,' Ruth murmured.

The vicar was back, looking grim. 'Er ... Martin ... I must talk to you,' he said.

Ruth asked, 'What is it?'

He cleared his throat. 'There's some problem ...' He indicated the undertaker's men. 'I'm afraid they won't handle the coffin.'

Ruth flinched as though she'd been struck. Nell put her arms around her mother and glared at the vicar. 'I expect they want "compensation" like the staff at the mortuary.' She raised her voice. 'That's how we got him loaded in.

Zipping him into some plastic bag like a piece of garbage!'

'How much?' Martin asked.

Stanhope stepped forward. 'We can do it, can't we? Between us?' Nell led Ruth inside while Bill, Morrie, Martin and the vicar slid the coffin out of the hearse, placed it on the undertaker's trolley and wheeled it towards the doors.

The vicar read the standard service to the six forlorn mourners, but Ruth's thoughts were elsewhere. She tried to remember a happy, vigorous Clive, but the pictures in her mind all reflected the last awful months. It all seemed, still, so utterly unreal – none of it more so than the bizarre manner of his death. From what Dr Singleton had told her of it, she felt nothing but gratitude towards the girl, Charlotte. The vicar's words gave her no comfort. Was this where it ended, then? With these empty phrases? He spoke of 'your servant . . . the dearly departed'; he said nothing about how Clive had lived or died. The righteousness, she thought, *the bloody righteousness* of his friends, his colleagues, his company, his community, his church. They had all shared the benefits of his hard work and generosity. But when he'd needed them, they'd broken him and walked away.

Nell and Martin sat on either side of her; she tightened her grip on their hands. The vicar prayed 'in the name of our Lord Jesus Christ'. What kind of Christianity was this? Whatever Clive's mistakes, he'd paid for them many times over. His disease had been incurable. Were cowardice and ignorance and bigotry also incurable?

The vicar droned on. 'I will say unto the God of my strength, why has thou forgotten me: why go I thus heavily, while the enemy oppresseth me? My bones are smitten asunder as with a sword: while mine enemies that trouble me cast me in the teeth. Namely, which they say daily unto me: Where is now thy God?'

161

The curtains behind the coffin parted, the remains conveyed into the inner chamber. Martin and Nell looked away, unable to bear it. Ruth forced herself to watch until the coffin was out of sight.

After an interminable time, Ruth found herself once again outside the building. She saw a figure moving hurriedly away, down the drive. 'It's Dennis,' Becca said. 'He was sitting in the back of the chapel; I saw him come in.'

'Why didn't he . . .' Ruth's voice trailed off.

'I guess he couldn't handle it. So . . . what now?'

'I don't know,' Ruth said numbly.

Martin put his arm round her. 'You can live again now, Mum.'

'I *have* been living,' she informed him, not unkindly. She turned to Stanhope. 'That girl . . . she didn't come. I wrote to her.'

'No . . . I was there yesterday. They said her father turned up and she left with him.'

'Well,' Ruth said weakly, 'I suppose that's it, then, isn't it? The end.'

Scott came over to her, clearly unnerved. 'See you around Ruthie.' He kissed her and turned abruptly away.

'Do you want a lift?' Martin asked.

'No, thanks. I'm going to walk this one off.' He started down the drive; Becca and Nell led Ruth towards the car, leaving Martin to say goodbye to Bill.

'Sharon's home from Switzerland,' Stanhope said.

'How is she?'

'She wants to be off again quite soon.'

'She's nice. I liked her, but . . . I don't think I took her seriously enough,' Martin admitted.

'Well, there were mitigating circumstances. You're both young. You've got lots of time.'

'I leave for Hong Kong in a couple of weeks.'

'Yes. Well . . . I'll tell her.' Stanhope paused, then

stretched out his hand. 'I'm sorry, Martin. For every-thing.'

'I know. We're all sorry. That doesn't seem to be enough, somehow. Does it?'

Momentarily united by their regrets, they shook hands and went their respective ways.

Ruth had tried to prepare herself for Clive's death, but nothing could have prepared her for the emptiness she felt when it actually happened. Until then, there'd been so much to do – much of it painful, but at least it had kept her busy. Now she awoke in the mornings dreading the days. For the first time in her life she had no appointments, no obligations of any kind. It was a terrifying, solitary kind of freedom. She felt cut loose from gravity, drifting away from the earth's friendly atmosphere into outer space.

It occurred to her that it was Thursday, the day when she used to go to the ballroom. Fleetingly, she considered the propriety of going dancing three days after her husband's funeral. She decided that propriety was irrel-evant. She couldn't think where else to go.

She stood in the doorway, surveying her former haunt in a kind of trance – not a chemically induced one this time. The band was playing a waltz; Edgar glided by with a partner and greeted her with a nod. She made her way to an empty table at the edge of the dance floor, wondering what exactly she was doing there, but feeling very much at home. Everything was exactly the same. Only she had changed.

The waltz ended and another began; Edgar stood over her, asking for a dance. He was an expert dancer; she relaxed in his arms, happy to follow his lead. 'Didn't I used to see you here before?' he asked.

She was astonished; were his partners all that inter-changeable. 'Of course you did, Edgar!'

'Ah, yes. I remember. Where's your friend, then? Who did the rumba?'

'She's away. In London. Seeing lawyers.'

'Oh, lawyers. *There's* a cross to bear. Tell you what – your other friend, the one with the little boy—'

'What about him?' she asked quickly.

'Is that who you came to see?'

'Yes,' she said. 'No.' She honestly didn't know.

'There's hundreds of liaisons here, you know. Age is no barrier.'

'It wasn't a liaison.'

'Well, he comes on Wednesdays now. He was here yesterday. With his little boy.' With Fraser? Surely it wasn't school holidays. 'Perhaps you'll see him next week, if you have time. You need to be retired, really, for this.'

'I am retired, I suppose.' She realised the truth of the words only as she spoke them. She'd completed her task and been pensioned off, she supposed. And now . . . what?

Edgar peered down at her face. 'You look a bit peaky.'

'Do I?'

'You've had a bereavement,' he said knowingly. 'I'm a dab hand at spotting it. I can tell them all in here. I'm bereaved myself.'

She gazed over his shoulder at the dancers; they all seemed so purposeful. 'I was married for twenty-five years,' she explained. 'I don't know what to do.'

'I wouldn't bother. Do what you fancy. You can always come here. I pop into the Waldorf in town, on Tuesdays, for a change. They do quite a decent tea-dance, too.'

He was kind, Ruth thought, and trying to be helpful – but she'd have to find her own answer. The band played the last bars of the waltz; she applauded perfunctorily, Edgar with great seriousness. 'Can I book you now for

164

the Slow Fox and the Viennese?' he asked with a rather quaint formality. 'I do Latin American with a woman over there . . . though I'd've made an exception for a rumba with your friend.' He started to smile, but caught himself. 'The Viennese can be relied on to give you a lift.'

He led her back to her table where she sat alone, watching the couples reforming for the tango. She watched enviously as the dancers, filled with purpose and passion, plunged into the dance.

Martin wanted to fulfill his legal and moral duties before he went back to Hong Kong, but he wasn't sure what those duties were. There was no one to tell him, and no one to help. His mother seemed indifferent to everything; his sister was never at home. Frustrated and confused, he turned up unannounced at Nell's studio.

She received him coolly. 'What do you want?'

'Oh, come on. I want to know how you are. You've not been home for three days.'

'I rang Mum,' she said defensively.

'I know. She told me.'

An unseen hand pulled a curtain behind Nell aside to reveal a scantily clad model and a photographer who peered curiously out at Martin. 'It's my brother,' Nell said. The young man Martin had seen in the publicity photo bounded over to Nell, threw a possessive arm round her and held out his hand. 'Pleased to meet you. I'm Nicky.' They shook hands and appraised each other intently. 'Hang about till I'm finished,' Nicky said, 'and we'll go for a drink.' He gave Nell a quick kiss and went back to his work, pulling the curtain shut behind him.

'Passion will flare up,' Nell said, 'even – or perhaps especially – under stress.'

'Stop it!' He sank into a chair, trying to pull himself together. 'I'm sorry. I'm trying to help Mum work things out. She's walking around in a bloody daze.'

'She'll come out of it. She did before.'

'At least you'll be around.'

'Not for long. I'm going to college.'

'Oh? Good idea! Re-sit your A-levels—'

'I'll never go near an A-level again, Martin. Someone should've stopped me the first time. You were "brilliant", remember? I was "good with people".'

'What then?'

'Photography, of course. They let me in with those.' She gestured across the room to a collection of enlargements in hinged frames: the photos she'd mounted for the exhibition. He walked over to inspect them. The first one was the close-up of Morrie, collapsing at the finish line of the race – a moving evocation of that unforgettable day. Martin turned to the next frame, and gasped. It was a collage of poignant studies of Clive, from the beginning to the end of his illness.

'You've come a long way,' he said admiringly. Nell recalled Clive using the same words about Ruth, when they'd watched her on television.

'You reckon?'

He nodded solemnly. 'This is good stuff.'

'I know how good it is.'

'Pity it wasn't used, really—'

'Oh, it will be used,' She assured him.

'Oh?' His lack of enthusiasm was obvious.

'It'll turn up in some photographic exhibition. Now Dad's actually died, I don't suppose the company will be so anxious to put me out of business.'

'In this area?' he asked hesitantly.

'What?'

'These photographic exhibitions . . .'

'What are you trying to say, Martin?' she asked, exasperated.

'Is there any point in going on attracting attention?'

She was indignant. 'This is my *work*!'

166

'You'll do more good work.'

'But not stuff that'll get you identified as the son of an AIDS victim?'

'I want to remember how he was before it happened.'

'You shouldn't,' Nell said, with no attempt at her usual flippancy. 'Because it made him larger. And her. And us. I wish he hadn't died. Especially in that way. But it wasn't a total loss, Martin.'

They both gazed at the several faces of Clive — one healthy, one agonised, one ravaged but apparently serene. Martin was the first to turn away.

Chapter 21

From the upstairs bedroom window of the townhouse, Ruth watched the men get out of the chauffeured limousine. One of them carried an enormous bouquet of white flowers. She heard the doorbell ring, heard Martin answer it and heard, a few minutes later, Martin's knock on her door. 'They're here, Mum.' She remained silently sitting by the window, staring at the empty street. She had neither the energy nor the words to express what she felt for the men downstairs.

Martin nervously ushered the men into the sitting room. 'She'll be down shortly,' he said. 'Please have a seat. What can I get you?' He took orders for gin all round, and began pouring.

The MD took the lead. 'She was a very good wife to your father. The strain these last months must have been intolerable.'

'She seems to have coped,' Martin said, handing him his drink.

'Thanks. I don't want to dwell on this, but your father's behaviour was, ah, uncharacteristic towards the end.'

'So I heard.' Martin passed drinks round to Geoff Harris and the rest of what had been Clive's 'team'.

'And it may have sent your mother off at a tangent too, slightly.'

Harris chimed in: 'She needs time to readjust.'

'That's just what I tell her,' Martin agreed.

The MD cleared his throat. 'We were obliged to take

certain measures. We didn't take them lightly. But if the company can do anything to help *now* . . . He was a valued member of the board.'

'And a terrific team leader,' Paddy said fulsomely. 'We all miss him.' There was a general murmur of agreement.

Martin could think of nothing to say except, finally, 'I have to go back to Hong Kong soon.'

'Banking, isn't it?' Harris was almost jovial.

'Yes.'

The MD felt himself on safer ground now. 'See us when you touch base again in London. Our banking connections are pretty comprehensive.'

'Thanks. What I was going to say was that I'd like to think there was a friendly eye kept on my mother. If there should be anything I need to know . . . My sister will be at college.

'Of course,' Marcus Blackstone assured him.

'Don't worry,' the MD said effusively. 'You're an impressive chap, Martin – no wonder your father was so proud of you.'

Martin's voice faltered. 'I'll, er . . . just see—' He darted out of the room and up the stairs to Ruth's door. 'Mum? You've got to see them! You knew they were coming!' He tried the door; it was locked. 'Mum,' he pleaded, 'they brought flowers . . .' He waited a moment, then made his way back downstairs. 'I'm sorry about this . . .' he said embarrassed.

The MD stood up and threw an arm round Martin's shoulder. 'No, no, no . . . we all understand. She's distressed.' He went on in a confidential, man-to-man tone. 'There's something we'd like you to remember. It could be that the circumstances of Clive's illness won't work to your advantage . . . in your career. Especially if you go into politics after all. We'll do all we can to see that you don't suffer.' His words were oblique, but his meaning was clear. 'With mutual discretion, I can't believe there'll be any problem.'

169

Martin nodded gratefully. 'I'm all in favour of discretion.'

'Good,' the MD said with an air of finality. 'And of course there are no material problems. Your sister could apply to our education scheme for a grant, by the way.'

'I'll tell her.'

The MD drained his glass; the others followed suit. 'I don't think we should intrude any longer,' Geoff Harris said significantly. The other men got thankfully to their feet.

'You're not intruding—' Martin protested just a beat too late.

'No, we'll say goodbye,' the MD insisted. 'And leave you all our sympathy.' Thus signalled, the men lined up to shake Martin's hand and offer the conventional condolences. As they did so, Martin heard the front door open. His sister appeared in the hallway, saw the men, their funeral suits and expressions, and glared with undisguised hostility. 'Sorry,' she said. 'Bad timing. I've a feeling I was supposed to have missed this.'

'Hello, Nell,' Geoff said. 'How are you?'

'Perhaps we won't go into condolences all over again,' the MD said hastily.

'No, don't.' She remained standing between them and the door; the glare intensified.

Paddy Firth tried to ease the tension. 'We feel it, too, Nell. Some of us were very close to your father.'

'I know,' she said, her voice low but perfectly clear. 'Screwed the same girl, I believe.'

The collective intake of breath was followed by a shocked silence. Martin finally collected himself enough to stammer apologies as the men said hasty goodbyes and pushed their way past Nell to make their escape. Martin saw them out to the car. Nell picked up the obscene bouquet and began to methodically rip it to shreds. By the time Martin returned to the sitting room, the floor looked as though it was covered with snow.

Bill Stanhope hadn't had a good night's sleep since he'd quit drinking. He resisted barbiturates, knowing that the insomnia would go when he resolved the questions about his future with which he'd been wrestling. Both he and Annie were painfully aware that drastic changes, professional and domestic, were imminent.

Throughout the twenty-eight years of his marriage, Bill's course had always been the one of least resistance. Annie made the decisions and willingly or grumbling, he went along. Now, with unprecedented decisiveness, he'd embarked on a path of his own, without consulting Annie or inviting her along. Annie fought for a restoration of the status quo, but Bill refused to fight: he merely withdrew into an impenetrable indifference. Annie pleaded, threatened, reasoned and cajoled – all to no avail. They still shared the same house but she felt as bereft as though he were a million miles away.

Not for the first time, she awoke at four a.m. in an empty bedroom and thought, *I can't go on living like this.* She could deal with anything, except this awful uncertainty. She would *demand* some explanations. Throwing on her dressing gown, she went to find him.

He was sitting by the window in the study, gazing out at the swimming pool; the end of his cigarette glowed in the dark. She knew he was aware of her presence behind him, but he didn't acknowledge it. 'I went to see Ruth,' she said.

He turned, but she couldn't make out his expression in the darkness. 'I'm not blaming you,' he said wearily.

'I made her some sort of apology. Look, it'll blow over . . .'

'People have long memories, you said.'

Annie switched on a lamp; Bill turned away. 'I don't suppose they'll *forget*,' she said, 'but she'll be accepted again. She's attractive. Some man might come along who—'

'—who can stomach the idea?' He took a picture post-card out of his pocket and handed it to her. The photo showed the harbour at Mykonos at night, with the lights of cruise ships glistening in the bay. The message said simply: *The view from the deck is the same.*

'Who's this from?' she asked. 'What does it mean?'

'Charlotte. Her father has a yacht, I believe.'

'Well, it wasn't *your* fault,' she said righteously. 'You did your best. *Some* people fall on their feet—'

He stood up and began to pace. 'She has a life-threatening disease. And I suspect *that* means she's back in the old routine.'

'Drugs?' Annie asked sharply. 'Was she on drugs when she did that to Clive? She was lucky she wasn't up on charges!' Bill faced her, seemed about to speak, then turned away. 'What? What is it?'

'There's a job going in Birmingham.'

She was aghast. 'Birmingham!'

'Head of a health centre, with attachment to a study group on urban environmental problems.'

'Is that what you want?'

'It would do. It would let me off a caseload of high blood pressure and strained jogging muscles.'

Annie felt as though she'd been kicked in the stomach. 'Give it time,' she pleaded. 'Please . . . don't do anything you'd regret. I'd regret. That's a consideration, isn't it? I like it here.'

Bill found himself longing for a drink, but resisted the temptation. 'I said I'd do something for him,' he said.

'You tried! The girl didn't want you to! She's crazy, Bill. None of it is your fault. He brought it on himself.' He didn't seem to be listening. 'Bill! What he'd really want is for Ruth and the children to get back what he took away from them. It's obvious. Listen, I did what you said.'

'What are you talking about?'

172

'In committee. It wasn't easy. Feelings are running pretty high in some quarters.'

'What did you say?'

'I said we should invite Ruth back. I told them that of course there's no chance of infection. The man's *dead*.'

She had his full attention now. 'And?'

'There was a lot of resistance. Half of them seem to think Ruth must be tainted, too, somehow. I was reminded that you're not the only doctor in the club. And there's the question of her other activities . . . getting involved . . .'

'Nobody's business but hers.'

'It went to a vote. Carried, by one.'

'Good.'

'"Good",' she mimicked, '"Good!" You needn't be so condescending – I'm not a child!'

'I'm sure it was the right decision,'

Seething with pent-up anger and frustration, she snarled, 'I've lost friends over this. That vote will never be forgotten. And Ruth was never any friend of mine.'

'I still think—'

'Here's a laugh for you,' she said bitterly. 'Whichever way you add up the points – and they were added up several ways, believe me – Clive has won this year's Warrender Trophy.' To her surprise, he did laugh. 'Madge Pearson wants to make the prize-giving a "reconciliation".'

'Isn't that reasonable?'

'I don't know! I don't know what's reasonable any more!'

Bill said 'I'm going to warm up some milk' and started towards the kitchen, effectively ending the conversation. She grabbed at his arm. 'When do you have to make a decision about Birmingham?'

'A month, six weeks . . .'

'If I say no,' she said, more frightened now than angry, 'will you go without me?'

Without answering, he shook off her arm and left the room.

Ruth stood in the drive of her family's house, postponing the moment of stepping inside. It was her first sight of the house since the day she and Clive and the children had moved out in defeat and disgrace. Now she felt only detachment, almost as though the people who'd lived there had been characters in a film she'd seen long ago. *What did I do here?* she wondered. She let Martin lead her inside, and realised he was waiting expectantly . . . for what? She looked around; someone, apparently under Martin's supervision, had restored everything to its pre-cataclysmic tidy, sparkling condition. The few pieces of furniture she'd taken with her to the townhouse were noticeably absent, but there were bowls of flowers every-where and no effort had been spared to make the house look homey and welcoming. Nell called out from the kitchen: 'I've put the kettle on.'

'Well?' Martin asked anxiously, 'what do you think?'

'It looks beautiful.' She followed him into the kitchen.

'They did a good job, didn't they – the agency people? With the garden, too. They did the heavy stuff – Mrs Gordon did the rest.'

'Mrs Gordon?'

'She wants to come back.'

Nell put the tea things on the table. 'She's poison. Do you know what she did? What she wrote?'

'She didn't understand,' Martin tried to explain. 'Most people didn't. We probably have to forget all that . . .'

'Why?' Nell asked, irritated.

'I'm only thinking of you, Mum.'

'Yes?' Ruth asked, wondering what he was leading up to.

'You could be back here in no time. What do you think?'

Her thoughts kept drifting. 'What?'

'About coming back?'

'Oh . . .'

'It's the obvious thing to do.'

'Why should she do the obvious thing?' Nell objected. Ruth tried to concentrate. 'It's so big, this house . . .'

'You needn't stay here long,' Martin said. 'It would just bring you back to base. You'd find your friends again.'

She smiled bitterly. 'Friends?'

Martin struggled to be patient; why was she making it so difficult for him? 'It *is* the obvious thing to do,' he repeated. 'God, Mum, I have to leave for Hong Kong tomorrow!'

She looked desolate. 'Yes, I know.'

'I'll okay the arrangements then?' He looked away from the pain and confusion in her eyes. 'Mum,' he said helplessly, 'in the end it'll just seem like any other death. No different from cancer, or heart disease.'

'It *was* different.'

'I think you should try to forget the difference as far as possible. Why don't you take a holiday when Nell starts college? Visit me; I'll show you Hong Kong. You could go on to New Zealand, and see Uncle Rob.'

Nodding vaguely, she wandered out of the kitchen and began to climb the stairs. Martin could feel his sister's accusatory stare burning into the back of his neck. He took a thick envelope from his pocket and slapped it on the table in front of her. 'Here,' he said belligerently, 'take a look at these.'

'What are they?'

'Bills: undertakers, contractors, solicitors. Check them, will you?'

'Why?'

'Because Mum won't,' he said, exasperated. 'She can't!'

Nell deliberately looked away. 'I'm sure you've done a good job as head of the household.'

'Nell,' he pleaded, 'I've got to leave tomorrow! What's wrong with wanting to see her settled?'

Nell shrugged. 'I like her unsettled, myself.'

'You won't be around.'

She made no apology. 'Okay. It's her choice.' She looked again at the kitchen. 'Fancy Mrs Gordon coming across. I'm surprised she didn't insist on fumigation!' She laughed, but something about the way Martin moved back into the hall, busying himself with the papers again, made her wonder. She followed him, the light dawning. 'Oh, Christ! You didn't, did you? You wouldn't. You *did*! You had the place fumigated! Just like any ignorant, sodding scaremonger—'

'Not fumigated,' he corrected her. 'Disinfected. You should be glad I thought about it. Somebody has to be realistic!' He felt painfully inadequate; whatever he did seemed to be wrong. He was only twenty-one, after all; what did they expect of him? His defences collapsed. 'I *was* scared,' he confessed. 'I'm still scared.'

His vulnerability moved Nell as his arguments had failed to do. 'She'll deal with it,' she assured him. 'Give her time.'

Their voices drifted upstairs, but Ruth took no notice. She stood in the centre of the bedroom she'd shared with Clive, as though in a trance. A cold winter light flooded the room; it looked immaculate and sterile. In a reverie, she touched the edges of familiar objects – a curtain, the dresser, the edge of the bed. She opened the wardrobe. The sight of the bare rail where Clive's clothes had hung triggered an avalanche of feelings; the full, unbearable weight of her loss swept the numbness of the past weeks irrevocably away. It wasn't only Clive that was gone. Their life together, some of it very good indeed, was gone. Till death us do part. And the part of her who'd been known only to Clive, by virtue of their years together – more than half of her life – that was gone, as well.

Forever. She felt a wrench, like an amputation. She'd thought she had no more tears; now a spasm of weeping engulfed her. She surrendered to it, knowing that these were tears of release – cleansing, wholehearted, restorative. Whatever might lie ahead, the nightmare was over.

Chapter 22

Madge Pearson's note was short, to the point, and cordial: on the basis of Clive's outstanding performance in a series of 'knockout' games last spring, he had been awarded the Challenge cup known as the Warrender Trophy. It would be presented on Friday evening at the annual club dinner; the membership sincerely hoped that Ruth would be there to accept it, and to resume her active participation in the women's committee. Madge had added a warm personal postscript, expressing her sympathy.

Ruth had no particular desire ever to see the golf club or any of its members again, but it did represent a kind of continuity, and she felt that she owed it to Clive to collect his trophy. Becca volunteered to accompany her, for moral support. But when Becca arrived at the townhouse to pick her up on the night, she seemed so distraught that for a moment Ruth wondered whether she might have been drinking. 'Come on in,' she said. 'I just have to comb my hair. I can't say I'm looking forward to this.'

'Nor am I. Shall we fortify ourselves with a drink?'

'What would you like?' Ruth asked nervously.

'What I'd *like* is whisky, but tomato juice is what I'll have, thanks. Unless you've got some hemlock.'

Ruth hadn't seen her since the custody hearing. 'How did it go?' she asked.

Becca looked despondent. 'It didn't take long.'

'Have they decided?'

Becca shook her head. 'They said I'll hear something soon.'

'What do you think?'

'I don't know how it's possible to tell. The lawyers stand up, they speak their lines, they sit down. That's what it's like, a play. No one's actually telling the truth. It's the performance that counts.'

'How was your performance?'

'Not good. I can't defend myself. Maybe it's because I'm indefensible.'

'Nonsense!'

'When they came up with what I was supposed to have done, my only real defence was that I was drunk at the time and couldn't remember. I don't think the judge was amused. There was one particularly bad moment,' she said bleakly. 'The other side produced a couple of photographs of the children. I hardly recognised them. It's been six months, and they're different people. Sarah's got those American braces on her teeth, and Michael's brushing his hair forward. And when my solicitor leaned forward to look, I caught the smell of gin. You know, that wonderful perfume—'

'You didn't—'

'No. But I've never wanted to more.'

'It's not over yet,' Ruth said. 'Let's drink to success.' Wryly, they raised their glasses of juice.

'What about you?' Becca asked. 'Are you going to sell the house?'

'Martin says this would be a bad time. I should hold on to it for a couple of years until it recovers its value.'

'Is that important?'

'Not to me. There's plenty of money for me. Only it's theirs, too, isn't it? Nell's and Martin's? Will be, eventually. I suppose I owe it to them to get the best out of it.'

'You're talking like the woman who used to live there,' Becca chided gently.

'Well . . . we all talk like that, don't we? We veer off sometimes, but we usually come back.' She drained her glass. 'I suppose we should go . . .'

The doorbell rang. 'I'm not expecting anyone,' Ruth said, and looked out of the window; a solitary figure stood there, head down, hands in pockets. 'It's Dennis!' she whispered, astonished. She hadn't seen him since the funeral, hadn't spoken to him since the night of . . . since the night. She felt awkward, slightly embarrassed and, most of all, angry. Becca remained discreetly in the sitting room while she went to the door.

'Aren't you going to say, "What are you doing here?"' he asked. He looked haggard and upset.

'What is it?'

'It's the kid. He's been put out of school.'

'Oh, no!' she said, dismayed.

'Little nurse with a big mouth told one of the mothers. Hysterics. We've got to start running again—'

'No,' she said instinctively. 'Don't.'

'—or else I've got to try talking them round. There's a meeting of parents . . .'

'When?'

'Tonight.'

Her response was automatic: 'Do you want me to come?'

'Would you?'

She hesitated. 'I said I'd accept Clive's trophy. At the club. The invitation was very . . . friendly. I thought I should give people a chance . . .'

Dennis flared up, incensed. 'Christ! If it's a matter of *honour*, forget it!'

Not for the first time, Ruth was struck by the resemblance between Dennis and his son; the same cobalt blue eyes, the sandy hair, the angular features. The vulnerability that showed on Fraser's face was well camouflaged on his father's, but Ruth knew it was there. She thought fleetingly of the scene that awaited her at the golf club and of the life it represented – an easy, circumscribed life that offered the illusion of safety.

When had she lost the ability to believe in it? It hadn't been all bad, that life, but she knew now, with absolute certainty, that whatever meaning it had held for her was gone. She said, 'You'd better come in.'

It took only a few minutes to explain the situation to Becca who immediately asked, 'Who else can we get to help?'

'I'll ring Nell. And Scott. Morrie won't come, but Scott will, if we can reach him.'

'I'll meet you there later,' Becca said, gathering her things. 'I've just remembered some business I've got to take care of.' In another moment Ruth and Dennis were alone, sitting in chairs at opposite ends of the room.

He looked at her sheepishly. 'I didn't come sooner because I didn't know what to say.'

'About Clive?'

'About you and me.'

'There wasn't anything to say, was there?'

'I could've said it was great,' he mumbled.

She hadn't expected that. 'Was it?'

'Yeah . . . 'course it was. Was it for you?'

'It was very good.' Her composure surprised them both.

'You're not . . . sorry about it? About going to bed?'

She smiled slightly. 'How refined you are, Dennis. Bed?' She glanced significantly over at the hearthrug.

'Aw, Jeez, come on, will you?' he squirmed.

'I'm glad,' she said calmly.

'You sure?'

'Yes. I've thought about it. I've made myself remember that Clive was dying at the time.'

'Aw, come on—'

'And in spite of that, I'm not sorry it happened.'

'Well . . . at least you know.'

Again, the faint smile; he couldn't quite make out its meaning. 'Yes. I'm grateful.'

'Look,' he said apprehensively, 'it was just bed, wasn't it? I mean, I'm not in any position to talk about the future—'

'Nor am I, Dennis.'

'So it's okay?'

'Of course. Of course it is.' She laughed. 'You don't have to marry me.' She reached for the phone.

Becca resolutely eschewed Dutch courage and sipped tomato juice throughout the club dinner and the tedious speeches that followed. The food tasted to her like sawdust, but it wasn't the food that she'd come for. It was a gala occasion – the event of the year, for which club and members were decked out with ostentatious care. Becca steeled herself; in her long career of creating scenes, this would be the first time she'd done so while cold sober.

'Well, there he goes, ladies and gentlemen,' boomed the MC, a Terry Wogan *manqué*, as yet another winner bounded onto the stage to collect his prize from the club president. 'Frank Barnett and the Maudsley Cup! No flies on Frank. All that, *and* he dealt with the flasher on the fourteenth green. Or . . . was *he* the flasher on the fourteenth green?' The audience, well-primed with alcohol, roared with laughter. Becca contemplated the table in front of her and waited. 'Now, going rapidly on, because time's running short and everyone wants to know who's this year's winner of the President's Cup. There's just a couple of things to be dealt with. The nine-hole award went to Douglas and Mary Gifford, who are in Kenya and unfortunately can't be with us tonight . . .' he waited for the flutter of applause to subside '. . . and the Warrender Trophy to Ruth Gregory, who has also had to send her apologies.' There was a faint murmur in the hall, and he continued. 'But now, on to the moment we've all been waiting for . . . tension mounting . . .'

Becca got to her feet. 'Excuse me,' she called out.

The interruption threw the MC off his stride. 'What's the problem?'

'That last item . . .'

'Yes?'

'I'm here to receive the Warrender Trophy, as a matter of fact.'

At the far table, Annie Stanhope glanced uneasily at her husband. In another part of the room, Geoff Harris shifted uncomfortably in his seat. The MC exchanged a worried word with the president and then spoke again into the microphone. 'That's absolutely in order, of course. So here's Becca Crichton, ladies and gentlemen, to receive the Warrender Trophy for Ruth Gregory'

Instead of applause, a hubbub of voices accompanied Becca as she made her way to the stage. The president handed her the trophy and the MC, himself applauding desperately, attempted to usher her off the stage. Becca walked to the microphone instead. 'Thank you very much, everyone,' she began, her voice clear and de-liberate. 'Ruth thought long and hard about accepting the invitation to prize-giving and, I think because it came at a time when she's particularly vulnerable and because of the kind of person she is anyway, she decided to accept this little gesture of welcome back into the fold. A fold that was nowhere to be seen when she most needed it—'

The MC reached for the microphone. 'Okay, Becca – you've made your point.'

She stood her ground. 'When she was looking after Clive, that is. Poor old Clive, he got caught in the most spectacular way, didn't he? Not just an ordinary dose of the clap, such as anybody – and I do mean anybody – might run into in these adventurous times. But the big one, the really big one!' Amidst shouts of 'Get her off!' she clung grimly to the microphone. 'As a matter of fact, Ruth can't be here tonight because she's trying to stop another wave of ignorance and cruelty from destroying a victim of the same disease. A victim even you couldn't help but call innocent. She won't be quiet, you see. She'll go on and on, talking about this, drawing attention to herself, making a fuss. So you'd better be absolutely sure that you mean welcome back—'

Outraged voices drowned her out as the MC and president joined forces to physically remove her from the stage, practically carrying her down the steps before they released her. She straightened up and walked slowly towards the door, amidst a deafening silence. Suddenly one person began to applaud. He got to his feet, still applauding. Annie Stanhope looked up at her husband with horror. 'Are you coming?' he asked, still applauding. She looked round at the watchful faces – the club members, many of them company men, and their wives. Hopelessly, she shook her head. Bill hurried across the room just in time to open the doors for Becca and follow her through them.

Ruth sat on the platform in the primary school hall with Nell, Dennis and the headmistress, while Dr Singleton made a reasoned plea on Fraser's behalf. She looked out at the worried faces of the parents, wondering what it would take to make them see that Fraser could be their child and that, like their children, he had a right to a normal life with his friends. The brightly coloured child-sized plastic chairs and children's paintings contrasted dramatically with the solemn expressions that confronted her. Scott sat inconspicuously in the back row, keeping a low profile. Morrie, whose Mediterranean tan had faded and was looking undeniably ill now, waited in the corridor.

Singleton was concluding his remarks. '. . . I'm going to repeat myself, because this fact is crucial: There is absolutely no evidence, in any of the studies that have been done in this country and in the United States, that anyone has been infected with the virus through the kind of casual person-to-person contact that occurs in schools.

'At times of crisis, people often respond by building walls around themselves when they should be coming together for understanding and support. We all have good reason to be afraid, for ourselves and for our children, but let's remember that the virus isn't the only danger; we're facing an epidemic of ignorance and prejudice, as well. Let's not mistake a child who needs our help for the enemy.'

Ruth couldn't tell whether the murmurs in the audience were hostile or friendly. The headmistress asked, 'Are there any questions you wish to put to the panel?'

A father got to his feet and spoke slowly, with emotion. 'Look, we're not hard. We're not monsters. But we're talking about our kids!'

'I know how you feel,' Ruth said, 'believe me.'

'Are you sure?' another father asked.

'Do you think I wasn't afraid for my own children?' Ruth asked. 'And for myself?'

A mother spoke up: 'And what about this business of the blood? You know what kids are, always cutting themselves, scraping their knees—'

'They never wash their hands if they can help it,' the first father chimed in. 'They lick the same ice creams.'

A woman in the back row called out, 'I feel sorry for the teachers, too! I think he should be taught on his own!'

'That's hardly practicable,' the headmistress said. 'Anyway, not one of my staff has complained.'

'He's already got haemophilia, for God's sake!' Dennis exclaimed. 'Give him a break, will you?'

'Sorry,' the first father replied, 'you've got an axe to grind. The risk is too great.'

Ruth leaned forward in her chair. 'The day Dr Singleton told us what was wrong with my husband, he said, "If the risk of infection were significant, I'd be dead by now".' She paused. 'So would I. So would my daughter. So would Fraser's father, here. And so would our friend Scott, who's looked after his partner constantly for the last two years. We're not dead. We're not even mildly ill, and the chances of our becoming infected with AIDS are more remote than the chances of our getting tuberculosis. Fraser is more at risk from your children than yours are from him. His immune system is damaged, and that means that catching a bad cold or flu might activate the virus, in which case he'd be much too ill to go to school anyway. If you isolate him you give him an extra problem, one that he needn't have. Keep in mind that you only know about this because an inexperienced young nurse who refused to handle him in hospital broke a confidence. If not for her, he'd still be working and playing beside your own children.'

The first father remained adamant. 'I don't see that we've any choice.'

'Yes!' Ruth insisted. 'Yes, you *have* a choice!'

The headmistress got to her feet. 'Thank you very much, Mrs Gregory.' She turned to the audience: 'I think what we should do now is ask our panel if they would leave us for a few minutes while we consider what they've had to say, and perhaps come to a decision about Fraser's place at school.'

Ruth moved with the others off the stage and down the aisle towards the exit, trying to make out the audience's mood. Morrie, Becca and Bill were waiting in the corridor. 'Did you convince them?' Becca asked.

Ruth turned to Singleton: 'Did we?'

'I don't know. Probably not. The same people, same faces, same minds . . .'

'There's a lot of them about,' said Becca.

Dennis banged his fist against the wall. 'Ah, Christ! That's us running again . . .'

Becca put a hand on his shoulder. '*Don't* run.'

'Who's going to teach him? Who's going to give him gold stars?'

'I don't know,' Becca replied, 'but there must be ways, and we have to find them.'

Singleton gestured towards the roomful of parents. 'How do you shift that ignorance?'

Nell said, 'The headmistress was with us.'

'Was she?' Ruth asked hopefully.

Morrie clutched Scott's arm and began to whimper. 'I want to go home. I want to—'

'Oh, shut it, for Christ's sake,' Scott snapped.

Ruth took Morrie's hand and held it tightly; it was dry and hot. 'It's all right,' she said soothingly. The doors to the meeting room swung open; surely it was too soon for a decision already, she thought. A couple emerged and hurried out, avoiding the eyes that followed them.

'Where you going, then?' Dennis called after them. 'Off for a hot bath and a good old scrub-down?'

Becca nudged Dennis with her elbow. 'Stop it!'

Ruth looked after the departing parents. 'That's not necessarily a bad sign. It means someone argued with them and they couldn't take it.'

'When we go back in,' Bill said, 'I'll have a go. The fact that I'm an ordinary doctor, not a specialist, might reassure them.'

'Yeah,' Dennis said enthusiastically, grasping at the straw. 'Anything! *Anything*!'

Nell felt obliged to warn Bill. 'The press is in there. You'll be reported.'

'That's okay,' he said, unperturbed.

Mentally sorting through strategies, Ruth turned to Singleton. 'We should try again with the information campaign.'

'Well,' Singleton shrugged, 'if you can face disaster over and over.'

Becca grinned. 'Disasters are my speciality. Count me

in.' Ruth, still holding Morrie's hand, held out her free hand to Becca, who took it gratefully. 'You look absolutely shattered,' she said. 'You must've used up a month's supply of adrenalin in there.'

'It's grief,' Bill said knowingly.

Becca sagged momentarily, reminded of her own demons, but then remembered what had transpired at the golf club, and brightened. 'Look what I've got for you!' she said to Ruth, reaching into her handbag and pulling out the Warrender Trophy. She glanced round the group and handed the silver cup to a surprised Morrie. 'On second thoughts, I'll let Morrie present it to you. If it gets round the golf club that *he's* held it, you won't have to give it back next year!'

In the tension of the moment, the black joke made them all laugh – a laughter that verged on hysteria. Once again, the door to the meeting room opened. The headmistress stepped into the doorway, her expression impossible to read. She said merely, 'We're ready for you now,' and stepped back into the room.

The laughter faded. No one moved, but all eyes were on Ruth. She stood up, touched Bill's arm and whispered urgently, 'Speak first, quickly, before they announce what they've decided. We might catch some of the doubtful ones.' To the others, she said, 'Everyone look optimistic. As if we expected to win.'

Bill, Becca, Dennis, Nell and Singleton rose, straightened themselves and looked to Ruth for their cue. She smiled encouragement. 'Come on,' she said. 'Follow me.'